FANTASIA GALORE

The inauguration of an annual selection of the "best" stories of a category is not an enterprise to be undertaken lightly. The field of pure fantasy, as distinguished from the tale of terror or the story of science fiction, has always had an ardent following, and in recent years a growing one. It is high time that the fiction of this marvel genre was commemorated regularly by a selection of its best.

DAW Books, whose publications of the *Annual World's Best SF* and *The Year's Best Horror Stories*, have proven popular, now launch the first of what we hope will be an annual pick of the best of fantasy fiction.

As to what we mean by fantasy, the most obvious evidence is in the names and reputations of the authors herein, which include Fritz Leiber, Robert E. Howard, Jack Vance, L. Sprague de Camp, and more.

And who could best be found to make this selection? None other than the man whose name has come to embody the concept of "adult fantasy," the renowned author, editor, and bibliophile, Lin Carter.

Enjoy it!

—D.A.W.

DAW BOOKS ANNUALS:

Edited by Donald A. Wollheim

Edited by Richard Davis

THE YEAR'S BEST
Fantasy
Stories

Edited by
Lin Carter

DAW BOOKS, INC.
DONALD A. WOLLHEIM, PUBLISHER

1301 Avenue of the Americas
New York, N. Y.   10019

DEDICATION

To the memory of the late

Hans Stefan Santesson

FIRST PRINTING, OCTOBER 1975

1 2 3 4 5 6 7 8 9

PRINTED IN U.S.A.

ACKNOWLEDGMENTS:

The Jewel of Arwen, by Marion Zimmer Bradley, first appeared as a brochure published by T-K Graphics, Baltimore, Md. It is reprinted here by arrangement with the author.

The Sword Dyrnwyn (orig. "The Sword"), by Lloyd Alexander, first appeared in the book collection, *The Foundling and Other Tales of Prydain* (1973; Holt, Rinehart & Winston): © 1973 by Lloyd Alexander. By permission of the author.

The Temple of Abomination, by Robert E. Howard, first appeared in the book collection, *Tigers of the Sea* (1974; Donald M. Grant, Publisher); © 1974 by Glenn Lord, administrator to the Estate of Robert E. Howard. By arrangement with Mr. Lord.

The Double Tower, by Clark Ashton Smith and Lin Carter, first appeared in *Weird Tales*, the issue dated Winter, 1973; © 1973 by Weird Tales. By permission of Leo Margulies.

Trapped in the Shadowland, by Fritz Leiber, first appeared in *Fantastic Stories*, the issue dated November, 1973; © 1973 by Ultimate Publishing Co., Inc. By permission of Fritz Leiber.

Black Hawk of Valkarth, by Lin Carter, first appeared in *Fantastic Stories*, the issue dated September, 1974; © 1974 by Ultimate Publishing Co., Inc.

Jewel Quest, by Hannes Bok, first appeared in *Kadath*, the first issue, dated 1974; © 1974 by Lin Carter.

The Emperor's Fan, by L. Sprague de Camp, first appeared in the book collection, *Astounding*, (1973; Random House); © 1973 by Random House, Inc. By arrangement with the author.

Falcon's Mate, by Pat McIntosh, first appeared in *Anduril*, July, 1974; © 1974 by John Martin and *Anduril*. By arrangement with John Martin.

CONTENTS

Introduction:

THE YEAR IN FANTASY

The world lost its greatest living master of fantasy in 1973 with the death of J. R. R. Tolkien. During his last years he had been working on the long-anticipated "prequel" to his masterpiece, *The Lord of the Rings,* a book to be called *The Silmarillion.* He does not seem to have completed his final revisions on this novel, unfortunately; but his son, Christopher Tolkien, is reportedly at work on the manuscript and is preparing it for eventual publication in a few years.

A few last works are known to exist, however, and the first of these, an interesting poem called *Frodo's Farewell to Middle Earth,* has appeared posthumously. A short work of fiction called *Mr. Bliss* is rumored to exist, and I understand that the fragment of a sequel (of sorts) to *LOTR* has been found, called *The New Shadow.* This is, most likely, only a "working title." Whether any other manuscripts will come to light in time is something which cannot now be foretold with any accuracy.

At the 1974 World Science Fiction Convention in Washington, D.C., a J. R. R. Tolkien Memorial Award for Achievement in Fantasy was announced. The award itself, popularly known as the "Gandalf," is a bronze statuette of Tolkien's beloved magician, created by the talented young fantasy sculptor, D. Enzenbacher. The first Gandalf to be awarded was a Grand Master award, given for an author's lifelong over-all contribution to the fantasy world: with singular appropriateness, the award was bestowed upon the late Professor Tolkien himself.

Fans of Sword & Sorcery in general, and of Conan the

Cimmerian in particular, suffered a setback during 1974 when the publisher of the Conan series, Lancer Books, suspended all publication. The loss to the field of this enterprising and prolific publishing firm is indeed grim; but the most frustrating thing about it may have been that Lancer cancelled all publications just before issuing the long-awaited final volume in the Conan series, *Conan of Aquilonia.* The four novelettes that were to have made up the contents of that book, however, have been appearing in Ted White's magazine, *Fantastic,* so at least the Conan buffs will know how the mighty Cimmerian brought to bay and finally destroyed his most cunning and tenacious adversary, Thoth-Amon the Stygian sorceror.

Another important publisher of fantasy, Ballantine Books, also came to the end of an era in 1974. The new management of the firm, which was recently sold to Random House, has begun to change the Ballantine image away from that of a quality genre publisher towards that of a mass-market paperback publisher such as Bantam or Avon. One of the first steps in this evolution was to terminate the Ballantine Adult Fantasy Series which had been a prodigious force in the rebirth of interest in fantastic literature. The last titles in the Series, which was launched under my editorship in 1969, will be *The Prince of Annwyn,* the fourth and final volume in Evangeline Walton's brilliant and beautiful retelling of the Four Branches of the Welsh *Mabinogion,* and the fourth of Katherine Kurtz' popular Deryni books, expected in 1975. No one regrets the demise of the Adult Fantasy Series more than I do, but at least it frees me for interesting new tasks such as the editorship of this new annual anthology series, *The Year's Best Fantasy.*

A modest number of new fantasy novels came out during the year, mostly from familiar authors of reliable abilities, such as Michael Moorcock, Poul Anderson and Andre Norton. But for most readers, and the great big wide and wonderful world of Real Books out there beyond the limited confines of our small genre, 1974 was the year of an explosive blockbuster of a book called *Watership Down* by an hitherto unknown writer with the uninspired name of Richard Adams. This odd item is being billed by the biggies of Criticdom as the *Iliad* and the *Odyssey* of the rabbits—you heard me, rabbits: it's about rabbits; yes, I said rabbits. Anyway, it's the first time I can remember when a fantasy novel got to the top of the *New York Times*' bestseller list (something neither Tolkien nor C. S. Lewis ever did, although I'm not so sure T. H. White didn't), and it shows every sign of turning into a Big Book on Campus and a cult classic just like Tolkien.

For those unable to take four hundred and twenty-nine pages of teensy-weensy type about rabbits, the year at least featured two new novels of unusual distinction. The first of these, by Poul Anderson, was an exciting and rather experimental *tour de force* set in a variant world in which William Shakespeare's two great fantasy plays, *The Tempest* and *A Midsummer Night's Dream*, would be considered sober and factual histories rather than imaginative extravaganzas. The novel is titled *A Midsummer Tempest*, and the cast of characters include King Oberon and Queen Titania, Puck, Prospero the Enchanter, Ariel and Caliban. Vieing for honors with the Anderson item as best new fantasy novel of the year, I would name a rousing and colorful piece of old-fashioned story-telling, *Merlin's Ring* by H. Warner Munn, one of the last books in the Ballantine Adult Fantasy Series. This vigorous and splendidly entertaining story concludes a series of Arthurian fantasies begun thirty-six years ago in the old *Weird Tales*.

Speaking of that magazine, the greatest of all the pulp magazines from the Golden Age of fantastic adventure fiction, *Weird Tales* began republishing recently, the first issue in the new series bearing the date of summer, 1973. Four issues of the resurrected magazine have thus far appeared, all under the capable editorship of Sam Moskowitz, who has succeeded in locating some previously unpublished fiction by a few of the great masters of the macabre who made *Weird Tales* famous. Among others, Moskowitz discovered an early tale by August Derleth, some previously unpublished stories by William Hope Hodgson, and coaxed a new story out of Carl Jacobi. *Weird Tales* also began running some new stories by Clark Ashton Smith, which I completed and put in final form.

The most recent issue of *Weird Tales* appeared midway into 1974; it was the fourth of the new series. Since then, however, declining sales and spotty distribution have forced the publisher, Leo Margulies, to suspend the magazine while he studies alternative ways of continuing the new series of *Weird Tales,* possibly as a paperback. The failure of this attempt to revive *Weird Tales* in its fiftieth year suggests that the age of the pulp magazine is finally over, and that an audience for such as *Weird Tales* simply can no longer be found.

With commercial publishers seemingly in the doldrums, it is interesting to contemplate the sudden rise of the small amateur publishers. These small specialty houses have been with us since 1939 when Arkham House, the grandaddy of them all, launched an uneven but vigorous career with the publication of *The Outsider and Others* by H. P. Lovecraft. The specialty houses have never been more active than they are right now, and their rise not only in the variety of their books and brochures, but in technical excellence and the sheer number of these publications certainly bodes well for the immediate future. The small houses have begun to mark out their individual territories, with former-bookdealer Donald M. Grant of Providence, R. I., specializing in the work of Robert E. Howard, former fanzine editor Jack L. Chalker going into bibliographies and commentaries on Smith and Lovecraft, etc., and long-time Philadelphia fan Ozzie Train beginning to reprint long forgotten fantasy novels in hardcover. With this activity coupled with such non-newsstand-distributed fantasy magazines as *Witchcraft and Sorcery, Whispers,* and my own new magazine, *Kadath,* the future of fantasy publishing may be seen entering into a new configuration.

With the suspension of Lancer and the gradual phasing-out of fantasy at Ballantine, just about the only market for original fantasy novels left is DAW Books. Don Wollheim auspiciously launched his new imprint with the publication of a collection of new short fantasies in Andre Norton's Witch World series, and since then has opened his list to include such Burroughsian borderline-fantasies as John Norman's Gor books, Alan Burt Akers' Prescot of Antares series, and my own Saga of the Green Star. He has further extended his range of publishing categories into real fantasy with my new Gondwane Epic and this new anthology series, *The Year's Best Fantasy.* Either he knows how to package and sell fantastic fiction where other publishers fail, or the readership for such is only large enough for one steady publisher. Time will tell.

—LIN CARTER

Hollis, Long Island, New York

THE YEAR'S BEST FANTASY

Marion Zimmer Bradley

THE JEWEL OF ARWEN

Although Professor Tolkien himself is no longer with us, other writers are already at work continuing his epic fantasy, or elaborating those matters he left undetailed. This story—little more than an episode—fills in a minor gap in our knowledge of Middle Earth by extrapolating from hints and clues in the great trilogy, producing a new narrative which throws light on the previously shadowy history of that gem which Arwen gave to Frodo in THE LORD OF THE RINGS, III, 252–253. Marion Bradley will be known to many readers for her vivid and adventuresome Darkover novels, which are deservedly popular; here she displays her expertise in Tolkienian lore. As the tale which follows has been previously published only in brochure form, with a limited printing, I imagine it will be unknown to most of you.

—LC

In the year of the fall of Osgiliath, great black Orcs appeared out of Mordor, and fearful indeed was the battle before that city. At that time Boromir, son of Denethor*, was the Eleventh Steward of Gondor; and a very great

---

*This was, of course, *not* the Boromir of the Fellowship, but his ancestor by some fourteen generations.

15

captain was he, wise and valiant in battle, fair and noble, beloved and feared. It is said that Boromir was the first to stand before the dread Witch-king, lord of the Nazgul, and seek to wound him with his sword.

Dreadful was their meeting, so that strong men fled like children or were cast down senseless in terror; but Boromir neither fled nor quailed, but struck boldly, slaying the Black Rider's fell steed, and ripping away with his sword the black mantle with which the Nazgul covered his hideous nothingness. And at last the Witch-king fled from before him; yet in that battle Boromir had suffered a wound from a Morgul-blade, and though it seemed, at first, a slight hurt indeed, from that day thence his arm withered and shrank in pain, and he fell into a wasting sickness. None of the wisdom of the healers of Gondor could aid him, though they were many; but while he lay sick in Minas Tirith, there came to the city Mithrandir, the Grey Pilgrim.

Boromir the Steward had ever welcomed the rare visits of this wisest of counsellors, and when Mithrandir heard that Boromir was like to die, he went up to see him, and asked to look at the blade which had wounded him; but when it was taken from the place where it had been laid away, lo—only the hilt remained. The Mithrandir looked grave and said, "There is no power in Gondor to heal this wound."

At this all men despaired, for Cirion, son of Boromir, was not yet of an age to sit in the seat of his father. But Mithrandir said that far up the great river Anduin, in the forest known as Lothlorien, there were those who might lend their aid; so Boromir was laid in a boat and, with a few of his household, borne up the stream to the crossing of Nimrodel; for in those days the journey was less perilous than later, though still set about with dangers.

And at the crossing of the Silverlode (for they were never fated to enter into the valley of Lorien), Boromir lay like a pale shadow, with no powers even to lift his head. And there they were met by the White Elf-Lord.

The White Elf-Lord greeted the company fairly and said that he had been sent from Lothlorien for their aid; at which they were astonished and afraid. Yet so kindly and wise he seemed that they quickly lost all fear and led him to Boromir, who lay like death and seemed not to know what befell him. Yet when the White Lord called him by name, he roused and spoke to him, at which they were all surprised; but they marked that his face was grave and angry. "This is the work of him I hate above all else in Middle Earth, save only the Enemy," he said, "and so deadly is this wound that it passes my skill, though indeed some ease from pain can I give this brave man." And he tended him with healing herbs and sang strange spells, and Boromir grew easier and seemed revived. Then the White Elf-Lord said, "Cruel is the journey to Imladris in the West, and long; hardly can this wounded man withstand that journey, yet I counsel him to undertake it, else he will swiftly pass away; not even into death which all men must endure, but to an evil and bitter bondage in the fell shadows whence this thing came to him. And he is too valiant and worthy a man to pass into that darkness; sooner would I see him slain."

Then the men of Boromir's escort took counsel, and it was resolved to bear him to Rivendell; and the White Elf-Lord went with them a part of the way, until Dimrill Stair was past, then rode ahead to bring word of their coming. Long and hard was that journey with the wounded man, yet Boromir was so staunch of heart, and so reluctant to pass into the darkness whereof the White Lord had warned him (for he had spoken in secret to him of this), that he endured it without complaint. And at last then he came to Rivendell, and there Elrond, who had more skill at such matters than any other master of wisdom, whether man or Elf, restored him beyond what any man would believe who had seen him lying like a shadow.

So Boromir dwelt for months in the house of Elrond, and returned slowly to strength of body and mind; and in that time he grew to a great friendship with the White Elf-Lord, who admired his bravery against their common enemy and grew to know him well in the days of his slow recovering.

But at last there came a day when the lord Boromir said, "Master Elrond, beyond all words is my gratitude to you; that man must be hard to please who could not abide content in this fairest of all houses forever, but beyond hope I have found healing for my deathwound; now must I take thought for my own land, and return to Gondor."

Elrond looked on him gravely and said, "In this valley you have found health, indeed, but that is not all due to my skill; there is virtue in Rivendell, that evil things have no power here. While you remain here the evil is stayed, though not banished—" and here he looked on Boromir's arm, which was still withered and shrunken to the size of a child's limb, though in all else he was recovered, "but if you depart hence it will not be so. A while you may continue, but your days will be shortened, and evil."

Boromir said without faltering, "If that indeed be my destiny, Master Elrond, then must I abide it as best I may. In such times as these, I may not leave my people fatherless. While a Steward of the House of Mardil keeps Gondor against the return of the king, peace there is in our land; and in my absence, so it be brief and at need while I seek healing, the High Warden rules in my stead. But should it be known that I propose to lay down my staff in good earnest and end my days elsewhere, then cruel would be the strife that would follow, and an end to such a peace as we have known. For those who have sworn fealty and service to the land follow me while I rule; but if no man justly claims power, again there will be a great struggle between those who will hold it. Strength shall be given me, I now judge, to set all in order; and then what shall follow, must follow."

Elrond smiled upon him. "Be it so, then," he said. "You men of Gondor, I can see, are strong in heart, worthy sons of the Faithful of Westernesse. And if fears for yourself do not keep you from your duty, I would not be willing that any words of mine should do so." And he took kind leave of Boromir and blessed him, and sent him with an escort of his household. But the White Elf-Lord travelled with the company a day's journey in friendship;

and when he made ready to say farewell he delayed for a moment and spoke apart with the Steward.

"Master Boromir," he said, "it grieves me to part with you, for it is not like that you will come northward again in such times, and now my folk do not travel in Ithilien or toward the South. I have thought long on what counsel I might give you that would ease the burden of what, I fear, must lie heavy on you in the days to come," and he looked up into the evening sky, where the early stars hung low, like diamonds. "This only will I say; when you walk in the court of the White Tree, take thought to the heirlooms of the Faithful."

"You speak to me in riddles," said Boromir, and the White Lord, laughing sadly, said. "Know you not yet that it is the way of my folk?" More he would not say, and they exchanged courteous words of farewell and parted, each hiding his sorrow.

So Boromir returned to his people and took thought to set all things in order. True had been the words of Elrond, for after he left the valley the pain and darkness came upon him often, though so mighty a man he had been that it was slow in returning. He could no longer grasp a sword in his shrunken hand; but he gave the command of the armies into the hands of his Warden and set his son Cirion, though he was still a stripling, in posts that should teach him to use power wisely. Farsighted was he, noble and high of heart, but even at the first he knew much suffering. Being most strong of will, he took little thought to himself; but one evening in great weariness he walked in the court of the White Tree, where the waters fell from the branches, and the words of the Elf-Lord came into his mind: *take thought to the heirlooms of the Faithful*. And as he looked up into the sky, there the seven stars of the Net swung low, and an old rhyme of lore of Westernesse came into his head in the ancient tongue:

> "Seven stars and seven stones,
> And one White Tree."

"Heirlooms," he thought. "What can that mean? The Horn of Mardil is our house's chief heirloom; yet it can be

little help. Nor my staff. Seven stars and seven stones—"
and he thought of the Stone of Minas Arnor, lying hidden
in a secret place, which not even the Kings of Gondor
dared to touch. Great was the peril of the Stones of Seeing: "And the White Lord would not counsel me to so
dread a course," he thought. Then as his eyes fell again
upon the stars he recalled how the White Lord had also
looked into the sky, and remembered the Seven Stars, the
jewels of light, whose brightness was a terror to all things
of darkness. Chiefest of these was the Star of Elendil;
worn by him in the Last Alliance when Sauron was
thrown down, and since then vanished in the North, so
men said. And now he recalled that indeed the House of
Mardil was one of those houses which held in their keeping one of the Seven Stars, preciously guarded as too high
and great even to be looked on, and not drawn forth for
many lives of men now, not indeed since the days of the
Kings. And suddenly a longing came upon him to look
upon the star. So he had it brought to him, a fair jewel
upon a fine chain of silver, and when he held it for a moment in his hand, suddenly it seemed that his pain was
gone, and the shadowy darkness cleared, as if a veil were
drawn away and he looked from a high place on clear
cloudless skies. He drew the first free breath in many
days; and when at last he turned again to the many duties
that lay upon him, his heart was clear of worry and fear.

From that hour, never again did he lay aside the jewel,
but wore it about his neck upon its chain. And those who
knew him well marked that when the look of drawn suffering came into his eyes he would lay his hand to it, and
be somewhat at rest.

Many and fearful indeed were his long sufferings, and
as the years drew on he grew withered and shrunken as a
man of thrice his years; yet where he had hoped at most
for two or three years to set his realm in order, he lingered for eleven years after his return from Rivendell;
and not in the highest hopes had he thought so much time
would be given to him. Weary indeed he was of life, and
long ere the end he longed to leave it, yet he clung to frail
strength remaining, until the year came when his son

reached full age and he knew he had achieved beyond his best hopes and there was no longer fear of strife within to mar their union against the strife from without. And then he quickly declined. No longer did the jewel bring any surcease from the pain within his ravaged limbs, but even now when he looked on it, some peace would come to his heart.

At last he lay near death, and he called his son Cirion to him and yielded up his Steward's staff and the horn that was the heirloom of their house. Then, after giving him counsel about the ordering of their country, he laid his hand to the jewel and said, "A precious thing has this been to our house, though less regarded than its worth till now, save as a thing of loveliness and a reminder of our lost glories. But I charge you now that you shall not keep it for yourself, for the time has come when it shall pass from the hands of our kindred. I desire you to send it North, by the trustiest messenger known to you, to come at last into the hands of Master Elrond of Imladris."

"It shall be done," said Cirion. "But why?"

"Great was his gift to me, and to you, and to Gondor, my son. For else you would never have reigned, nor another Steward sat here to await the return of the King. And it comes to me that you will bear this staff for many years.* Yet no gift would Master Elrond accept from me, and few gifts of men would be worthy. Now I deem—" and here the foresight of his fathers came upon him, "— that the time has come when such a gift shall not be ill-given; for the shadow shall fall even on the beauty of Imladris and the glory of fair Lothlorien, and the arts of Elrond shall strive in vain. Alas that he who has healed so many hearts of their grief shall know the cruellest of sorrows when all his skill shall fail." And so saying he died.

In those days, now and again, one would still go secretly from Gondor northward to the forests of Lorien; and into

---

*He bore it, in fact, for eight-and-ninety years of men; and in his time the Rohirrim came to the Mark.

the hands of one such, Cirion entrusted the White jewel. So it was brought to Lorien, to be sent by the Lady Galadriel to Rivendell when occasion should offer. But the jewel abode in Lorien for many years of men (which were but as a brief time to the Elven-folk) and then, by chance as men say, the sons of Elrond abode for a time in Lorien; and when they set out Westward, the White Lord journeyed in their company and into his hands the star jewel was given.

(Here ends the first part of the narrative which has been translated. It has been told elsewhere that less than twenty years after the death of Boromir, the shadow indeed fell on the house of Imladris. A portion of the narrative which follows is written in what appears to be an attempt to transpose into the Common Tongue a song of the form and metre of some of the very few remaining Elvish songs. No attempt has been made to give more than the briefest summary of the lay, and no claims are made for the authenticity of any part of the tale; it is simply presented until those entrusted with the true story shall come forth. It has elsewhere been told how the Lady Celebrian, journeying to Lorien, was delayed in the Redhorn Pass by a storm through which their beasts could not pass; and while they waited there for the passing of the snow, they were attacked with dreadful suddenness by Orcs out of Moria, who scattered and slew her escort and carried the Lady into darkness.)

It has been said of the Sons of Elrond that they were like to their father: fair and grave, courteous and wise. Often had they ridden to battle with the captains of the North, and they were great captains of men and terrible in war, yet wise in counsel and gentle of speech, and much loved by those who knew them. Many were their friends among the men of the North-Kingdom, and there was even a jesting byword (so like was one to the other) that a most long-lived chieftain was one who had "lived long enough to learn to tell Elrohir from Elladan."

And indeed they were alike; save that if one spoke in company, whether in counsel or jest, it was likest to be

Elrohir, for Elladan was the more silent, though as wise and brave.

Word had come to Lothlorien that Celebrian had set out on her way, and her sons set out to meet her, in company of the White Lord, being fearful of the delay. They came at last to one of her escort lying near death in the pass and heard the tale; and in great grief and fear, they made swift plans. The White Lord was to ride in search of the scattered escort, hoping to bring rescue swiftly. Elrohir meanwhile drew off the main Orc body by a daring feinted attack; a desperate plan and one from which he escaped only hardly and by chance with his life; while Elladan went down alone into the darkness of Moria in search of his mother. And save for the overthrowing of Sauron whereby Gil-galad perished, this has been called one of the bravest deeds of any of the Elven-kind; but in after years, so great a pain was this memory that never would the house of Elrond allow any song of it to be sung in Imladris or in Lorien.

But before the three parted on their fearful errand, the White Lord gave in haste to Elladan a jewel like a star. "No time there is to prepare a better light for that fell darkness, and your sword alone will not serve," he said; "Yet this may serve you better than any other light." And so it was; for the light of that jewel, though not great, held a terror for the Orc-folk even greater than the burning pain of the Elven blades. And when it blazed upon them out of their familiar darkness they fled before it in dread, blinded; so that ever after, in the minds of all that folk, the image of terror was that of a tall elf-warrior bearing a sword of painful light and another, more dreadful, light at his breast. So at last Elladan, after a time he could never reckon (for even Elven-folk lose all sense of time in such caverns) came to Celebrian, slew her tormentors, and bore her, still living though wounded with a poisoned dart and evilly tormented by the Orcs, to safety above ground.

Terrible was that journey to Imladris and the home-coming, and indeed the shadow that fell upon the Valley then. Elrond healed her wounds indeed; but for the Lady of Rivendell, who had dwelt all her life within the refuges of Imladris and golden Lorien, there was in them no extraordinary virtue of healing. So that the other hurts of that deadly wound and deadly torment came on her with a greater swiftness than on any mortal folk, and swiftly she darkened and fell into great weariness. And they knew she must soon depart over Sea into the West, or else depart forever into a greater parting.

Yet she herself was reluctant to go, for such partings of kin are sadder to Elves than ever to men; and for near a year she lingered among them, and much she endured. And for all this time she wore the white jewel which had brought them safely out of the darkness, and so it came to pass as Boromir of Gondor had foreseen that this was a precious gift to the house of Elrond. For this was one of the Seven Stars given into the hands of those who passed from Numenor ere it was cast down, and held by the highest of the Edain in exile; and in it was preserved a gleam of the true light.

But at last, when the leaves of that year were falling, Elrond would permit her to delay no longer, and they bore her to the Havens. Heavy was it now upon Elrond and Galadriel that they were pledged to abide the long strife in Middle Earth, for it seemed in that hour that they were weary past telling of their abiding here. And Elrohir and Elladan vowed that every Orc east of the mountains should know the terror of the sons of Elrond.

Bitterest of all was her parting from Arwen; for although as yet no shadow of the doom of Luthien had fallen upon Arwen Evenstar, yet Celebrian foresaw it in that hour; though she parted from her kindred for long years of Middle Earth, going before them into the long home of her people, from Arwen the parting should endure past the ending of the world. Greater still was the lamenting of Arwen; for though she had dwelt for many years on the green earth, still she was but a young maiden in the reckoning of her people and had known no griefs; nor had she any great tasks set before her, to give strength in that hour.

And so even among her manyfold sufferings Celebrian strove to appear light of heart, and at last she held in her hand the star-jewel, shining forth as if indeed her fingers could not hide it, and "I shall need this no more," she said, "for where I go that light is undiminished. Its virtue is less for our kind than for men who must ever dwell beyond that light and so are greatly strengthened even by its palest gleam; yet even for us, Arwen, though it gives little healing, great is the ease of the heart which lies in its brilliance, when sadness and fear and dark thoughts and memories are upon the heart. And of these I foresee you will have full measure, and wait long for your happiness; maybe as long as I must wait till I be all glad again." Then she looked on the White Elf-Lord as if asking leave, and he smiled in consent, hiding that he too was wrung with grief; and she said, "Be comforted, Evenstar; wear this, which was first worn by a brave mortal, recalling that even the short-lived find courage to endure their griefs without hope. And when you look on it, remember that I dwell in the light of which this is the palest memory, and that this gleam was light to my heart in this saddest of leaf-fallings." Then she clasped the jewel about Arwen's throat where a moment it lay like a burning star, and then as if its light was slowly fading into cloud, grew paler and soft. And softly she said, but as in jest, "This is not the Elfstone which one day will come to you, Evenstar, so wear this well until the other is yours to look upon for your heart's peace. And in that hour, when you have won through the shadows to splendor, and after long doubt and sadness come at last to joy, then yield up this jewel to one whose need is greater in that hour, as I to you." But Elrond looked grave and said, "Peace; speak not of that," so she said no more, and they parted.

So Celebrian departed over Sea, and for many years the songs of Rivendell were silent and even the Hall of Fire was dark . . .

It is told elsewhere of Arwen that even as her brothers did she grow in grace and wisdom, bright and blessed among the great ladies of Elf-kind, and only the Lady Galadriel was fairer or more beloved. And it is known that in the hour when at last she achieved her heart's desire, and sat in joy beside the King Elassar, did she indeed yield up to the Ring-Bearer, in his need, the White Jewel of the Star.

Lloyd Alexander

THE SWORD DYRNWYN

Speaking of Tolkien, the one newcomer to the fantasy ranks most often mentioned in the same breath with him is Lloyd Alexander. His Prydain books, a series of six marvelously entertaining novels, are much the same sort of stuff as Tolkien's towering masterpiece: vigorous, magical, heroic, filled with spectacularly imaginative scenery, yet focusing on human nature and real people and honest emotions. They rank high on my list of the best fantasies published since THE LORD OF THE RINGS. Last year, Lloyd returned to Prydain for one last, nostalgic visit, and returned with a bookful of new tales, of which this one is my favorite.

—LC

When Rhitta was crowned King of Prydain, the great sword Dyrnwyn, fairest ever wrought, was given him in token of his kingship. Its hilt was gem-studded, its blade forged in a secret way of which the knowledge had been long lost. On its scabbard were graven these words: *Draw Dyrnwyn, only thou of noble worth, to rule with justice, to strike down evil. Who wields it in good cause shall slay even the Lord of Death.* Of Dyrnwyn's lore and lineage little was known. King Rhydderch Hael, sire of King Rhych, and grandsire of Rhitta, had been the first to bear it, and it was said a deep enchantment had been laid upon it. So Rhitta, in his turn, bore Dyrnwyn as a weapon of power and protection over the land.

One day Rhitta and his nobles rode to the hunt. In the heat of the chase, Rhitta galloped across the field of the old shepherd, Amrys, and by mishap broke the gate of his sheepfold.

In dismay, Amrys called out to Rhitta:

"King, I pray you, mend my gate. My arms are too weak, my hands tremble, and I have no strength to set new posts and raise it again."

In his eagerness to follow the chase, Rhitta hastily answered:

"Shepherd, this is a small matter. You have my word it will be made right."

With that, seeing his nobles had gone on ahead, Rhitta spurred his horse after them. All day he hunted and at nightfall rode back weary to his castle. There his councilors awaited him with such pressing business and so many urgent questions that he forgot his promise to the shepherd.

Next morning, however, as Rhitta rode out hawking, at the portal stood the shepherd holding a young lamb in his arms.

"King, mend my gate," cried Amrys, clutching Rhitta's stirrup. "Already my sheep have strayed, all but this one lamb."

"Have I not given you my word?" answered Rhitta sharply, angry with himself at forgetting, but angrier still that the shepherd dared reproach him before his nobles. "Yours are small cares and will be set right in good time. Trouble me no longer with them."

The hawk on the King's wrist beat her wings impatiently. Rhitta kicked his stirrup free of the shepherd's hand, shouted for his hunting band to follow, and galloped on his way.

That night, with plates filled and wine flowing, Rhitta feasted in his Great Hall. Amid the laughter and boasting of his warriors and the music of his harpers, Rhitta had no thoughts for his promise to the shepherd.

Next day, Rhitta held court with all his councilors and his war leader to consider matters of policy and high state. In the midst of the council, pulling free of the guards who tried to hold him back, Amrys hobbled into the throne room and fell on his knees before the King.

"King, mend my gate," he cried, holding out the body of the lamb. "I have honored you as a worthy king and upright man, but now my sheep are lost and, for want of its mother, my lamb is dead."

"Shepherd," warned Rhitta, "I commanded you to trouble me no more. How dare you come into my council? Grave affairs are being weighed here."

"Sire," answered the shepherd, "is it not a grave thing when a king's promise goes unkept?"

"What, shepherd," Rhitta burst out, "do you tell me I have been false to my word?"

"No, sire," the shepherd returned simply, "I only tell you that so far it has not been kept."

Rhitta's face reddened at being so reproved, and he rose angrily from his throne to answer:

"Shepherd, mind your tongue! Do you call your king an oath-breaker?"

"You say it, sire, not I," replied Amrys.

These words of the shepherd so kindled his wrath that Rhitta drew his great sword and struck down Amrys. But then, when his rage lifted and he saw he had slain the old man, Rhitta was filled with remorse; he flung aside the weapon and covered his face with his hands.

However, his councilors gathered around him and said:

"Sire, that was a grievous deed. Nevertheless, the shepherd brought it on himself. He gave you a mortal insult, calling you a liar to your face. This affront to Your Majesty could have grown to treason and open rebellion. You could have done nothing else."

At first Rhitta had blamed only himself, but the more his councilors spoke, the more their words eased his mind and he saw the matter in their light. So, putting aside his regrets, he willingly agreed:

"Yes, it is true and clear to me now. I did only my duty. Even so, to show I bear no grudge, see to it the shepherd's wife and family are given each a purse filled with gold and the finest ram and ewe of my own flock; and never are they to want for anything whatsoever."

All the court hailed Rhitta's wisdom and generosity. But that night in his bed chamber, when he laid aside his weapons, on the bright scabbard of Dyrnwyn he saw a dark stain, the black of dried blood. Try as he would to wipe the scabbard clean, the dark stain remained.

Next day, his Chief Councilor came and told him:

"Sire, we would have done your bidding, but the shepherd has neither wife nor family. Indeed, he has no kindred to inherit his land."

Rhitta's war-leader, hearing this, came forward and said to the King:

"Sire, it has been your custom to reward those who serve you well. Before, when land was left without an heir, you bestowed it on other lords. Will you give this holding to me?"

Rhitta hesitated, weighing the war-leader's request but thinking, too, how well the shepherd's land would increase his own domains. Then he said:

"The shepherd affronted me. It is only justice that his land be added to mine."

"Justice?" retorted the war-leader. "The King's justice well serves the King's ends."

Rhitta turned angrily upon him and exclaimed:

"It will be as I said. How dare you question me? Do you reprove your King? Take warning from the shepherd's fate."

"Do you threaten a companion's life?" the war-leader flung back, his lips white with rage. "Know, Rhitta, you have a warrior to deal with, not a weak old man. You, sire, take warning yourself."

At this, Rhitta struck the war-leader across the face and cried:

"Be gone! Do you covet more land? For your insolence, your own lands are forfeit. I banish you from court and castle, and from all my realm."

Seeing Rhitta's fury, neither the councilors nor any of the nobles dared gainsay the King. So the war-leader was sent away in disgrace and his place given to another.

That night in his bed chamber, when he laid aside the sword, Rhitta saw the stain had not only darkened but spread until it covered still more of the scabbard. Again he tried to wipe it away, but the stubborn stain remained and grew larger. Alarmed, he gave the weapon to his master swordsmiths, but even they could not scour it clean.

Now, at this same time, many nobles, witnesses to the

war-leader's disgrace, began muttering among themselves. The King's injustice rankled them, and they feared his wrath might fall heavily upon them, too, and strip them of their own lands and honors. So they swore to rise against the King and overthrow him.

But Rhitta had word of their plan, and even as they gathered to do battle, Rhitta and his war band rode out and set upon them, taking them by surprise.

As it happened, the place of battle was none other than the field of Amrys, the shepherd. And Rhitta, leading his warriors, suddenly cried out in horror. There, before his eyes, stood the shepherd, bloody with wounds, holding out the lamb to him.

The King's warriors, seeing nothing, took Rhitta's outburst as a battle cry. They galloped to a fierce charge, slew most of those who stood against them, and put the rest to flight.

Rhitta, however, had reined his horse and turned from the fray. With all speed, he rode back to his castle and lay trembling in his chamber, certain the shepherd had meant to work some evil upon him.

When his warriors brought him word of the victory and asked if he had been wounded and therefore had not led the onslaught, Rhitta dared not speak of what he had seen. Instead, he told them he had been stricken with a sudden fever and sickness. But he could not keep the shepherd from his thoughts.

"He deserved his fate," Rhitta repeated to himself. "As do all who have risen against me. Let their lands, too, be forfeit, and their goods and gold be added to the royal treasure."

But now the stain spread farther and blotted nearly all the scabbard. Again Rhitta ordered his swordsmiths to find a means of scouring it. They could not.

"The metal is flawed," Rhitta cried. "The sword is ill-made."

At the same time, uneasiness filled his mind. Now he believed the sight of Amrys had been an omen and a warning of more treachery. And so he called his councilors, war-leader, and captains of his war bands, saying:

"All our enemies are not yet overcome, and the danger to the kingdom is even greater. The kinsmen of those traitors will surely seek vengeance. It may be they plot against me even now. It may be they bide their time, waiting for a day when they shall rise and strike me unawares. Better that I crush them before they can rally in strength and set upon me."

So Rhitta commanded his war bands to arm and at dawn be ready to seek out the traitors' kindred and to slay them.

That night, however, Rhitta turned and tossed on his couch, and long before dawn he woke at the sound of a voice murmuring in his chamber. He started up, sweating in terror, to see the shepherd, holding the lamb in his arms, standing at the foot of the couch. And Amrys spoke and said:

"Remember the broken gate, sire. Remember the lost sheep. The path you follow leads you, too, astray. Mourn the dead by pitying the living."

The shepherd would have spoken further, but Rhitta, unheeding, sprang up with a great cry, seized Dyrnwyn, and made to snatch the blade from its sheath. But the scabbard held the blade with jaws of iron. In fear and rage, Rhitta clawed at the weapon and tore at it until his fingers were bloodied. He could not draw the sword.

When his guards ran to him with torches, he ordered them away, saying only that he had had a bad dream. But in the morning, while his warriors stood by their horses, awaiting him to mount and ride at the head of the battle host, Rhitta summoned his war-leader and told him:

"I have thought on this, and see it is not fitting for a King to show concern in such a matter. Were I myself to lead the host, there would be those to say I judged the danger greater than it is, or even that I had no trust in my officers. Therefore, go and do my bidding as it seems best to you, in any way you choose."

Then Rhitta withdrew to his chamber, never daring to tell the true reason behind his words.

It is written on the scabbard, thought Rhitta, *Draw Dyrnwyn, only thou of noble worth.* Since the blade will not come freely to my hand, my warriors may believe their King is unworthy to rule.

The more he stared at the inscription, the more the words of it mocked him. With a curse, Rhitta seized a dagger and tried to scratch away the graven message. Though he marred some of the letters, the engraving remained and stood out all the brighter against the scabbard. Then Rhitta flung aside the dagger. Clutching the sword, he crouched trembling in a corner of his chamber, his eyes glittering feverishly, his glance never at rest.

Soon his war-leader came to him and said:

"Sire, the kinsmen of our enemies are slain, and all their families, their wives and mothers, their children, and any who might claim blood-kinship with them."

Rhitta nodded vaguely, as if he had not heard, and murmured:

"You have done well."

Afterward, Rhitta looked again at Dyrnwyn. It had turned altogether black.

That night, although he slept behind barred and bolted doors, he woke to the sound of weeping and once more saw the shepherd, who turned an anguished face upon him and called out:

"Sire, find yourself before you lose yourself."

Rhitta stopped his ears against these words, but even the coming of day did not dissolve his nightmare, and the empty chamber echoed the shepherd's weeping.

"Another omen," cried Rhitta. "Another warning that all my enemies are not yet slain. All must be found and killed, or I shall lose my kingdom."

So he commanded his war bands to hunt down any who had ever befriended the kinsmen of his enemies; any who spoke in favor of them; and any who did not praise the worthiness of his kingship.

Even this brought him no peace. While Rhitta stayed in his chamber, his warriors roved the kingdom unchecked, putting many to the sword, with or without cause, having more thought now to seizing treasure than finding treachery. However, instead of striking terror in the hearts of Rhitta's foes, such deeds only enraged them and gave them the courage of despair. Where before there had been few, now arose many who joined to fight against the King. And Rhitta's nightmares, instead of easing, grew more terrible. He feared to stay alone in his chamber and feared to leave it, sure some hand would strike him down even amid his bodyguard.

So Rhitta commanded new chambers made for him deep underground, with heavy doors and thick walls. At the same time he ordered his henchmen to stand circling his couch with drawn swords and keep watch over him.

Now, each night, Rhitta slept in a different chamber. Not even his councilors could be certain where to find him. Next he commanded other rooms to be built, with hallways, tunnels, and galleries, winding and crossing, twisting and turning, in a pattern he alone could fathom. Thus the stronghold became known as Spiral Castle.

Even then Rhitta was unsatisfied. He commanded his builders to dig still deeper, until they could go no farther. There they hewed a chamber out of living rock, in which he heaped great stores of provisions, treasures of gold and goods, coffers of jewels, robes of rich fur, and stacks of finely wrought weapons. He raised a high couch where he lay with the black sword at his hand. At last Rhitta was content. No enemy could find him, no battle host breach the walls. Even so, he ordered his warriors to stand about him with naked blades.

That night he went easily to sleep. But soon, as before, anguished murmuring aroused him. There stood the shepherd, his wounds running red, staining the fleece of the lamb he carried.

The warriors, sure no danger was possible, had fallen asleep on the floor. Rhitta would have cried an alarm, but his voice turned to stone in his throat as Amrys drew closer.

"Wretched King," came the shepherd's sorrowing voice, "Alas, you would not heed me. You slew me once for a broken gate; but you have slain yourself a hundred times over. King, I pity you as I would pity any suffering creature."

The shepherd reached out a hand as if he would touch Rhitta's brow.

Seeing this, fearing that Amrys meant to strike him, Rhitta found his voice again and shrieked in terror. At the same time, bending all his might, straining every sinew in a final effort, he clutched the hilt of Dyrnwyn and strove to rip it from the scabbard. He shouted in triumph as the blade came free.

But he had unsheathed only a hand's breadth of the blade when tongues of white flame burst crackling from the hilt and all the length of the scabbard. Where before he had been unable to draw the weapon, now he could not unclench his fists and cast the blazing sword away.

Like a lightning bolt, the flame filled the chamber in an instant, striking down even the guards who staggered to their feet. Then, as suddenly as it had risen, the flame was quenched. Still gripping the blackened sword in his lifeless hands, King Rhitta fell back on his couch. And all was silent.

Because no one could find a way through the tunnels and galleries, Rhitta lay as he had fallen. In time, having no word of him, his councilors and courtiers at last knew him to be dead.

And only the shepherd Amrys ever grieved for him.

Robert E. Howard

THE TEMPLE OF ABOMINATION

Although Robert E. Howard died at thirty, so prolific a writer of stories was he that even today, nearly forty years after his demise, previously unknown or unpublished tales are still coming to light. The story which follows next is one of these: part of a cycle of four historical adventure yarns (only one of which was published anywhere), it has only recently been discovered and printed. Howard had nearly completed this yarn before laying it aside, for some reason we will probably never know. The last seven hundred words, added to finish the story off, are the work of Richard L. Tierney.

—LC

"Easy all," grunted Wulfhere Hausakliufr. "I see the glimmer of a stone building through the trees. . . . Thor's blood, Cormac! are you leading us into a trap?"

The tall Gael shook his head, a frown darkening his sinister, scarred face.

"I never heard of a castle in these parts; the British tribes hereabouts don't build in stone. It may be an old Roman ruin—"

Wulfhere hesitated, glancing back at the compact lines

of bearded, horn-helmeted warriors. "Maybe we'd best send out a scout."

Cormac Mac Art laughed jeeringly. "Alaric led his Goths through the Forum over eighty years ago, yet you barbarians still start at the name of Rome. Fear not; there are no legions in Britain. I think this is a Druidic temple. We have nothing to fear from them—more especially as we are moving against their hereditary enemies."

"And Cerdic's brood will howl like wolves when we strike them from the west instead of the south or east." said the Skull-splitter with a grin. "It was a crafty idea of yours, Cormac, to hide our dragon-ship on the west coast and march straight through British country to fall on the Saxons. But it's mad, too."

"There's method in my madness," responded the Gael. "I know that there are few warriors hereabouts; most of the chiefs are gathering about Arthur Pendragon for a great concerted drive. Pendragon—ha! He's no more Uther Pendragon's son than you are. Uther was a black-bearded madman—more Roman than Briton and more Gaul than Roman. Arthur is as fair as Eric there. And he's pure Celt—a waif from one of the wild western tribes that never bowed to Rome. It was Lancelot who put it into his head to make himself king—else he had still been no more than a wild chief raiding the borders."

"Has he become smooth and polished like the Romans were?"

"Arthur? Ha! One of your Danes might seem a gentle-woman beside him. He's a shock-headed savage with a love for battle." Cormac grinned ferociously and touched his scars. "By the blood of the gods, he has a hungry sword! It's little gain we reivers from Erin have gotten on his coasts!"

"Would I could cross steel with him," grunted Wulf-here, thumbing the flaring edge of his great axe. "What of Lancelot?"

"A renegade Gallo-Roman who has made an art of throat-cutting. He varies reading Petronius with plotting and intriguing. Gawaine is a pure-blooded Briton like Arthur, but he has Romanish leanings. You'd laugh to see him aping Lancelot—but he fights like a blood-hungry devil. Without these two, Arthur would have been no more than a bandit chief. He can neither read nor write."

"What of that?" rumbled the Dane. "Neither can I . . . Look—there's the temple."

They had entered the tall grove in whose shadows crouched the broad, squat building that seemed to leer out at them from behind a screening row of columns.

"This can be no temple of the Britons," growled Wulfhere. "I thought they were mostly of a sickly new sect called Christians."

"The Roman-British mongrels are," said Cormac. "The pure Celts hold to the old gods, as do we of Erin. By the blood of the gods, we Gaels will never turn Christian while one Druid lives!"

"What do these Christians?" asked Wulfhere curiously.

"They eat babies during their ceremonies, it is said."

"But 'tis also said the Druids burn men in cages of green wood."

"A lie spread by Caesar and believed by fools!" rasped Cormac impatiently. "I laud not the Druids especially, but wisdom of the elements and ages is not denied to them. These Christians teach meekness and the bowing of the neck to the blow."

"What say you?" The great Viking was sincerely amazed. "Is it truly their creed to take blows like slaves?"

"Aye—to return good for evil and to forgive their oppressors."

The giant meditated on this statement for a moment. "That is not a creed, but cowardice," he decided finally. "These Christians be all madmen. Cormac, if you recognize one of that breed, point him out and I will try his faith." He lifted his axe meaningfully. "For look you," he said, "that is an insidious and dangerous teaching which may spread like rust on the wheat and undermine the manhood of men if it be not stamped out like a young serpent under heel."

"Let me but see one of these madmen," said Cormac grimly, "and I will begin the stamping. But let us see to this temple. Wait here—I'm of the same belief as these Britons, if I am of a different race. These Druids will bless our raid against the Saxons. Much is mummery, but their friendship at least is desirable."

The Gael strode between the columns and vanished. The Hausakliufr leaned on his axe; it seemed to him that from within came a faint rattle—like the hoofs of a goat on a marble floor.

"This is an evil place," muttered Osric Jarl's-bane. "I thought I saw a strange face peering about the top of the column a moment agone."

"It was a fungous vine grown and twisted about," Black Hrothgar contradicted him. "See how the fungus springs up all about the temple—how it twists and writhes like souls in torment—how human-like is its appearance—"

"You are both mad," broke in Hakon Snorri's son. "It was a goat you saw—I saw the horns that grew upon its head—"

"Thor's blood," snarled Wulfhere, "be silent—listen!"

Within the temple had sounded the echo of a sharp, incredulous cry; a sudden, demonic rapping as of fantastic hoofs on marble flags; the rasp of a sword from its scabbard, and a heavy blow. Wulfhere gripped his axe and took the first step of a headlong charge for the portals. Then from between the columns, in silent haste, came Cormac Mac Art. Wulfhere's eyes widened and a slow horror crept over him, for never till this moment had he seen the steel nerves of the lean Gael shaken—yet now the color was gone from Cormac's face and his eyes stared like those of a man who has looked into dark, nameless gulfs. His blade dripped red.

"What in the name of Thor—?" growled Wulfhere, peering fearfully into the shadow-haunted shrine.

Cormac wiped away beads of cold sweat and moistened his lips.

"By the blood of the gods," he said, "we have stumbled upon an abomination—or else I am mad! From the inner gloom it came bounding and capering—suddenly—and it almost had me in its grasp before I had sense enough to draw and strike. It leaped and capered like a goat, but ran upright—and in the dim light it was not unlike a man."

"You are mad," said Wulfhere uneasily; his mythology did not include satyrs.

"Well," snapped Cormac, "the thing lies upon the flags within; follow me, and I will prove to you whether I am mad."

He turned and strode through the columns, and Wulfhere followed, axe ready, his Vikings trailing behind him in close formation and going warily. They passed between the columns, which were plain and without ornamentation of any kind, and entered the temple. Here they found themselves within a broad hall flanked with squat pillars of black stone—and these indeed were carved. A squat figure squatted on the top of each, as upon a pedestal, but in the dim light it was impossible to make out what sort of beings these figures represented, though there was an abhorrent hint of abnormality about each shape.

"Well," said Wulfhere impatiently, "where is your monster?"

"There he fell," said Cormac, pointing with his sword, "and—by the black gods!"

The flags lay bare.

"Moon-mist and madness," said Wulfhere, shaking his head. "Celtic superstition. You see ghosts, Cormac!"

"Yes?" snapped the badgered Gael. "Who saw a troll on the beacon of Helgoland and roused the whole camp with shouts and bellowings? Who kept the band under arms all night and kept men feeding the fires till they nearly dropped, to scare away the things of darkness?"

Wulfhere growled uncomfortably and glared at his warriors as if to challenge anyone to laugh.

"Look," said Cormac, bending closer. On the tiling was a wide smear of blood, freshly spilt. Wulfhere took a single glance and then straightened quickly, glaring into the shadows. His men bunched closer, facing outward, beards a-bristle. A tense silence reigned.

"Follow me," said Cormac in a low tone, and they pressed close at his heels as he walked warily down the broad corridor. Apparently no entrance opened between the brooding, evil pillars. Ahead of them the shadows paled and they came forth into a broad circular chamber with a domed ceiling. Around this chamber were more pillars, regularly spaced, and in the light that flowed somehow through the dome the warriors saw the nature of those pillars and the shapes that crowned them. Cormac swore between his teeth and Wulfhere spat. The figures were human, and not even the most perverse and degenerate geniuses of decadent Greece and later Rome could have conceived such obscenities or breathed into the tortured stone such foul life. Cormac scowled. Here and there in the sculpturing the unknown artists had struck a cord of unrealness—a hint of abnormality beyond any human deformity. These touches roused in him a vague uneasiness, a crawling, shuddersome half-fear that lurked white-maned and grisly at the back of his mind . . .

The thought that he had briefly entertained, that he had seen and slain an hallucination, vanished.

Besides the doorway through which they had entered the chamber, four other portals showed—narrow, arched doorways, apparently without doors. There was no altar visible. Cormac strode to the center of the dome and looked up; its shadowy hollow arched above him, sullen and brooding. His gaze sought the floor on which he stood and he noted the pattern—of tiling rather than flags, and laid in a design the lines of which converged to the center of the floor. The focus of that design was a single, broad, octagonal slab on which he was standing . . .

Then, even as he realized that he was standing on that slab, it fell away silently from under his feet and he felt himself plunging into an abyss beneath.

Only the Gael's superhuman quickness saved him. Thorfinn Jarl's-bane was standing nearest him and, as the Gael dropped, he shot out a long arm and clutched at the Dane's sword-belt. The desperate fingers missed, but closed on the scabbard—and, as Thorfinn instinctively braced his legs, Cormac's fall was checked and he swung suspended, life hanging on the grip of his single hand and the strength of the scabbard loops. In an instant Thorfinn had seized his wrist, and Wulfhere, leaping forward with a roar of alarm, added the grasp of his huge hand. Between them they heaved the Gael up out of the gaping blackness, Cormac aiding them with a twist and a lift of his rangy form that swung his legs up over the brink.

"Thor's blood!" ejaculated Wulfhere, more shaken by the experience than was Cormac. "It was touch and go then . . . By Thor, you still hold your sword!"

"When I drop it, life will no longer be in me," said Cormac. "I mean to carry it into hell with me. But let me look into this gulf that opened beneath me so suddenly."

"More traps may fall," said Wulfhere uneasily.

"I see the sides of the well," said Cormac, leaning and peering, "but my gaze is swiftly swallowed in darkness . . . What a foul stench drifts up from below!"

"Come away," said Wulfhere hurriedly. "That stench

was never born of earth. This well must lead into some Roman Hades—or mayhap the cavern where the serpent drips venom on Loki."

Cormac paid no heed. "I see the trap now," said he. "That slab was balanced on a sort of pivot, and here is the catch that supported it. How it was worked I can't say, but this catch was released and the slab fell, held on one side by the pivot . . ."

His voice trailed away. Then he said, suddenly: "Blood —blood on the edge of the pit!"

"The thing you slashed," grunted Wulfhere. "It has crawled into the gulf."

"Not unless dead things crawl," growled Cormac. "I killed it, I tell you. It was carried here and thrown in. Listen!"

The warriors bent close; from somewhere far down— an incredible distance, it seemed—there came a sound: a nasty, squashy, wallowing sound, mingled with noises indescribable and unrecognizable.

With one accord the warriors drew away from the well and, exchanging silent glances, gripped their weapons.

"This stone won't burn," growled Wulfhere, voicing a common thought. "There's no loot here and nothing human. Let's be gone."

"Wait!" The keen-eared Gael threw up his head like a hunting hound. He frowned, and drew nearer to one of the arched openings.

"A human groan," he whispered. "Did you not hear it?"

Wulfhere bent his head, cupping palm to ear. "Aye— down that corridor."

"Follow me," snapped the Gael. "Stay close together. Wulfhere, grip my belt; Hrothgar, hold Wulfhere's, and Hakon, Hrothgar's. There may be more pits. The rest of you dress your shields, and each man keep close touch with the next."

So in a compact mass they squeezed through the narrow portal and found the corridor much wider than they had thought for. There it was darker, but further down the corridor they saw what appeared to be a patch of light.

They hastened to it and halted. Here indeed it was lighter, so that the unspeakable carven obscenities throng ing the wall were cast into plain sight. This light came in from above, where the ceiling had been pierced with several openings—and, chained to the wall among the foul carvings, hung a naked form. It was a man who sagged on the chains that held him half erect. At first Cormac thought him dead—and, staring at the grisly mutilations that had been wrought upon him, decided it was better so. Then the head lifted slightly, and a low moan sighed through the pulped lips.

"By Thor," swore Wulfhere in amazement, "he lives!"

"Water, in God's name," whispered the man on the wall.

Cormac, taking a well-filled flask from Hakon Snorri's son, held it to the creature's lips. The man drank in great, gasping gulps, then lifted his head with a mighty effort. The Gael looked into deep eyes that were strangely calm.

"God's benison on you, my lords," came the voice, faint and rattling, yet somehow suggesting that it had once been strong and resonant. "Has the long torment ended and am I in Paradise at last?"

Wulfhere and Cormac glanced at each other curiously. Paradise! Strange indeed, thought Cormac, would such red-handed reivers as we look in the temple of the humble ones!

"Nay, it is not Paradise," muttered the man deliriously, "for I am still galled by these heavy chains."

Wulfhere bent and examined the chains that held him. Then with a grunt he raised his axe and, shortening his hold upon the haft, smote a short, powerful blow. The links parted beneath the keen edge and the man slumped forward into Cormac's arms, free of the wall but with the heavy bands still upon wrists and ankles; these, Cormac saw, sank deeply into the flesh which the rough and rusty metal envenomed.

"I think you have not long to live, good sir," said Cormac. "Tell us how you are named and where your village is, so it may be we might tell your people of your passing."

"My name is Fabricus, my lord," said the victim, speaking with difficulty. "My town is any which still holds the Saxon at bay."

"You are a Christian, by your words," said Cormac, and Wulfhere gazed curiously.

"I am but a humble priest of God, noble sir," whispered

the other. "But you must not linger. Leave me here and go quickly lest evil befall you."

"By the blood of Odin," snorted Wulfhere, "I quit not this place until I learn who it is that treats living beings so foully!"

"Evil blacker than the dark side of the moon," muttered Fabricus. "Before it, the differences of man fade so that you seem to me like a brother of the blood and of the milk, Saxon."

"I am no Saxon, friend," rumbled the Dane.

"No matter—all men in the rightful form of man are brothers. Such is the word of the Lord—which I had not fully comprehended until I came to this place of abominations!"

"Thor!" muttered Wulfhere. "Is this no Druidic temple?"

"Nay," answered the dying man, "not a temple where men, even in heathenness, deify the cleaner forms of Nature. Ah, God—they hem me close! Avaunt, foul demons of the Outer Dark—creeping, creeping—crawling shapes of red chaos and howling madness—slithering, lurking blasphemies that hid like reptiles in the ships of Rome—ghastly beings spawned in the ooze of the Orient, transplanted to cleaner lands, rooting themselves deep in good British soil—oaks older than the Druids, that feed on monstrous things beneath the bloating moon—"

The mutter of delirium faltered and faded, and Cormac shook the priest lightly. The dying man roused as a man waking slowly from deep sleep.

"Go, I beg of you," he whispered. "They have done their worst to me. But you—they will lap you round with evil spells—they will break your body as they have shattered mine—they will seek to break your souls as they had broken mine but for my everlasting faith in our good Lord God. He will come, the monster, the high priest of infamy, with his legions of the damned—listen!" The dying head lifted. "Even now he comes! Now may God protect us all!"

Cormac snarled like a wolf and the great Viking wheeled about, rumbling defiance like a lion at bay. Aye, something was coming down one of the smaller corridors which opened into that wider one. There was a myriad rattling of hoofs on the tiling—"Close the ranks!" snarled

Wulfhere. "Make the shield-wall, wolves, and die with your axes red!"

The Vikings quickly formed into a half-moon of steel, surrounding the dying priest and facing outward, just as a hideous horde burst from the dark opening into the comparative light. In a flood of black madness and red horror their assailants swept upon them. Most of them were goat-like creatures, that ran upright and had human hands and faces frightfully partaking of both goat and human. But among their ranks were shapes even more fearful. And behind them all, luminous with an evil light in the darkness of the winding corridor from which the horde emerged, Cormac saw an unholy countenance, human, yet more and less than human. Then on that solid iron wall the noisome horde broke.

The creatures were unarmed, but they were horned, fanged and taloned. They fought as beasts fight, but with less of the beast's cunning and skill. And the Vikings, eyes blazing and beards a-bristle with the battle-lust, swung their axes in mighty strokes of death. Girding horn, slashing talon and gnashing fang found flesh and drew blood in streams, but protected by their helmets, mail and overlapping shields, the Danes suffered comparatively little while their whistling axes and stabbing spears took ghastly toll among their unprotected assailants.

"Thor and the blood of Thor," cursed Wulfhere, cleaving a goat-thing clear through the body with a single stroke of his red axe, "mayhap ye find it a harder thing to slay armed men than to torture a naked priest, spawn of Helheim!"

Before that rain of hacking steel the hell-horde broke, but behind them the half-seen man among the shadows drove them back to the onslaught with strange chanting words, unintelligible to the humans who strove against his vassals. So his creatures turned again to the fray with desperate fury, until the dead things lay piled high about the feet of their slayers, and the few survivors broke and fled down the corridor. The Vikings would have scattered in pursuit but Wulfhere's bellow halted them. But as the horde broke, Cormac bounded across the sprawling corpses and raced down the winding corridor in pursuit of one who fled before him. His quarry turned up another corridor and finally raced out into the domed main cham-

ber, and there he turned at bay—a tall man with inhuman
eyes and a strange, dark face, naked but for fantastic
ornaments.

With his strange short, curved sword he sought to parry
the Gael's headlong attack—but Cormac in his red fury
drove his foe before him like a straw before the wind.
Whatever else this high priest might be, he was mortal, for
he winced and cursed in a weird tongue as Cormac's long
lean blade broke through his guard again and again and
brought blood from head, chest and arm. Back Cormac
drove him, inexorably, until he wavered on the very brink
of the open pit—and there, as the Gael's point girded into
his breast, he reeled and fell backward with a wild cry . . .

For a long moment that cry rang up ever more faintly
from untold depths—then ceased abruptly. And far below
rose sounds as of a grisly feast. Cormac smiled fiercely.
For the moment, not even the inhuman sounds from the
gulf could shake him in his grim fury; he was the Avenger,
and he had just sent a tormentor of one of his own kind to
the maw of a devouring god of judgement . . .

He turned and strode back down the hall, to join Wulfhere and his men. A few goat-things passed before him in
the dim corridors, but fled bleating before his grim advance. Cormac paid them no heed, and presently rejoined
Wulfhere and the dying priest.

"You have slain the Dark Druid," whispered Fabricus.
"Aye, his blood stains your blade—I see it glowing even
through your sheath, though others cannot, and so I know
I am free at last to speak. Before the Romans, before the
true Celtic Druids, before the Gaels and the Picts, even,
was the Dark Druid—the Teacher of Man. So he styled
himself, for he was the last of the Serpent-men, the last of
that race that preceded humanity in dominion over the
world. His was the hand that gave to Eve the apple, and
set Adam's foot upon the accursed path of awakening.
King Kull of Atlantis slew the last of His brethren with the
edge of the sword in desperate conflict, but He alone survived to ape the form of man and hand down the Satanic
lore of olden times. I see many things now—things that
life hid but which the opening doors of death reveal! Before Man were the Serpent-men, and before them were
the Old Ones of the Star-shaped heads, who created mankind and, later, the abominable goat-spawn when they

realized Man would not serve their purpose. This temple is the last Outpost of their accursed civilization to remain above ground—and beneath it ravages the last Shoggoth to remain near the surface of this world. The goat-spawn roam the hills only at night, fearful now of man, and the Old Ones and the Shoggoths hide deep beneath the earth till that day when God mayhap shall call them forth to be his scourge, at Armageddon . . ."

The old man coughed and gasped, and Cormac's skin prickled strangely. Too many of the things Fabricus said seemed to stir strange memories in his Gaelic racial soul.

"Rest easy, old man," he said. "This temple—this *Outpost,* as you call it, shall not remain standing."

"Aye," grunted Wulfhere, strangely moved. "Every stone in this place shall be cast into the pit that lies beneath!"

Cormac, too, felt an unaccustomed sadness—why he knew not, for often had he seen death before. "Christian or no, yours is a brave soul, old man. You shall be avenged . . ."

"Nay!" Fabricus held up a trembling, bloodless hand; his face seemed to shine with a mystic intensity. "I die, and vengeance means naught to my departing soul. I came to this evil place bearing the cross and speaking the cleansing words of our Lord, willing to die if only this world might be purged of that Dark One who has so foully slain so many and who plotted the Second Downfall of us all. And God has answered my prayers, for He has sent you here and you have slain the Serpent; now the Serpent's goat-minions can but flee to the wooded hills, and the Shoggoth return to the dark bowels of Hell whence it came." Fabricus gripped Cormac's right hand with his left, Wulfhere's with his right; then he said: "Gael—Norseman—fellow humans you be, though of different races, different beliefs . . . Look, now!" His countenance seemed to shine with a strange light as he feebly raised himself on one elbow. "It is as our Lord told me—all differences between us pale before the menace of the Dark Powers—aye, we be all brothers . . ."

Then the mystic, far-seeing eyes of Fabricus rolled upward and closed—in death. Cormac stood in grim silence, gripping his naked sword, then drew breath deeply and relaxed.

"What meant the man?" he grunted at last.

Wulfhere shook his shaggy mane. "I know not. He was mad, and his madness led him to his doom. Yet he had courage, for did he not go forth fearless, even as goes the berserker into battle, careless of death? He was a brave man—but this temple is an evil place that were better quitted . . ."

"Aye—and the sooner the better!"

Cormac sheathed his sword with a clang; again he breathed deeply.

"On to Wessex," he growled. "We'll clean our steel in good Saxon blood."

Clark Ashton Smith

THE DOUBLE TOWER

Like his friend Robert E. Howard, the late Clark Ashton Smith also left among his papers the manuscripts of unpublished or unfinished stories, and notes and titles and outlines for many tales which he did not live to write. I have obtained permission from his Estate to complete several of these, and to turn some of Smith's notes and outlines into finished tales, crafted in what I earnestly hope to be a reasonable facsimile of his ornate and lapidary prose. This is the second of these "posthumous collaborations" to be published; very appropriately, it adorned the pages of the recently revived Weird Tales, *where so many of Smith's bizarre fantasies were first published.*

—LC

Requiring solitude wherein to pursue his study of the antique goeties, Zloigm, premier archimage of the race of sentient ophidians which immediately preceded man in the dominion of this planet, turned from the teeming, basaltic warrens of his kind to the desolate and uninhabited plateaux of the interior of the primordial continent of the serpent-men. There, among steep scarps of glittering obsidian, cleft by vertiginous chasms whose silence was riven only by the intermittent spouting of geysers, he found at last the solitude which he desired. Where fuming volcanic peaks soared to pierce the zenith, on a flint-strewn plain which shuddered ever to interminable subterranean convulsions, he caused to be raised his lonely tower of ebon glass by the bitter shores of a black tarn, and commenced his studious inquiries into the most abstruse and recondite of the elder thaumaturgies.

Fundamental to the acquisition of this wisdom was the forbidden science of necromancy, and in the practice of this penumbral and gruesome craft had Zloigm become proficient to a superlative degree. From the indistinct lips of the spectres of the most celebrated of primordial mages, conjured hence by his art from remote and fabulous bourns, he wrung the most jealously guarded formulae and litanies, and the secrets of the most legendary of the pentacles and sigils of lost antiquity which had lapsed from mundane knowledge aeons before. Those phantoms which proved stubborn or disobedient to his will he cowed with the threat of certain spiritual rigors and torments, or else prisoned within the surface of a mirror of black steel where they must dwell forever, trapped in a hell of two dimensions only, until they repented of their obduracies and yielded up to Zloigm the cantrips or invocations or liturgies of which he required knowledge.

Betimes, for greater convenience, he fleshed such phantasms within gaunt and umber mummies transported to his lone and solitary abode from many a hidden crypt, or buried vault, or lost and immemorial necropolis, by powerful genii bound subservient to his word. And many the frightful secret of an age-forgotten demonology was hoarsely whispered to him by the dry, worm-fretted lips of some withered lich, wrapped in dusty cerements redolent of ancient spices and the sharp mineral stench of tomb-natron, which housed the captive ghost of some prehistoric wizard of repute. On yet other such occasions, a spirit thus conjured up from the depths of time was forced to vivify a cunningly contrived automaton of sparkling brass, or grotesque idols of rough-hewn and porous lava, magically rendered capable of audible speech.

Over the lapse of interminable years, having by these means exhausted the arcana of the purely mundane sorcerers of extinct civilizations of the forgotten prime, Zloigm eventually came to cast his questing spells yet

further afield. And into his conjurational circle he summoned the spiritual essences of weird and monstrous beings—ultra-telluric magi which dwelt on distant planets
remote in either time or space, or made their abode in
the husks of burnt-out stars, or within the radioactive
nuclei of certain far-wandering comets. So adept had the
ophidian necromancer become by this time in the tedious
and exacting art of the invocation of spirits, and to so
adroit and subtle and profound a magistry had he attained, that it was not only within his power to summon up the apparitions of the dead, but of the living as
well, whose astral or spectral counterparts he could force
to him even across the untold distances of interstellar or
trans-galactic space. And many and unthinkably alien
were the bizarre abnormalities he called to his circle for
due questioning. Some there were who, in their normal
sphere, were accustomed to go about on two legs, or
four, or six; and some that lacked the pedal extremities
entire, and slithered on their bellies in the quaking slime
like unto gigantic worms, or swam in the perpetual night
that reigns in the uttermost depths of nameless seas, or
drifted aloft forever on the eternal winds of storm-lashed
worlds upon untiring and rigid pinions of animate crystal.

With one extra-terrestrial intelligence in particular did
the necromancer desire to hold converse. He had learned
of its existence from a race of sagacious arthropods who
dwelt in caverns beneath the crust of a frozen satellite
which revolved about the double star Pornox in the con-
stellation of the Mantichora. The insectoid sages spoke of
this being (whom they knew by the unpronounceable
name, Crxyxll) in the most enthusiastic terms, for they
held its attainments in the arcane philosophies in the highest esteem. They described it to Zloigm as an intelligent
crawling white mould, which was the lone and solitary
denizen of an otherwise deserted world circumambulant
to a dim and nigh-extinguished sun called Klr, which
was situated in the very remotest of the spiral nebulae,
in those regions adjacent to ominously rumored Shaggai
which lies near the ultimate verge of angled space.

The sentient Crxyxll, however, proved obdurate in the
extreme and Zloigm was forced to employ the most dire
and stringent modes of persuasion at his command; but
the philosophic mould succeeded in resisting every con-

juration in the grimoire of the necromancer. At length, grown frustrate by the obstinacy of the mould-entity, Zloigm cast aside all prudence and sonorously intoned a ritual of such supernal and transcendent authority as to command even the presence of one of the Elder Gods. As he enunciated the monstrous cacophonies of this frightful incantation, the heavens darkened ominously; the ivory moon veiled her pallid visage in mist, as if reluctant to attend the ultimate blasphemy, and the wan and timid stars fled, one by one, from the nocturnal zenith. Beneath the audacious necromancer the earth shuddered and the very foundations of his tower groaned aloud as if in protest: but naught deterred the ophidian from the consummation of the ritual.

There soon materialized before Zloigm a dim luminance, a haze of light, a blur of phosphoric ectoplasm which floated, insubstantial as a vapor, within the triply drawn Circle of Power. But albeit his endeavors at invoking the spirit of the mould-savant had at last eventuated in success, naught Zloigm could do would force the apparition into speech. To his several attempts to extract from the recalcitrant Crxyxll the ultimate arcana of his magistry, the phosphorescent spectre preserved a truculent and adamantine silence.

In vain did the ireful necromancer threaten the entity with the Yggrr incantation, the Nn'gao elixir, and with nine periapts carven from the ivory teeth of pterodactyls. Likewise did it remain obdurately silent before the Scarlet Sign, the Z light, and the Chian games. Even the curse-litany of Glorgne, which he recited in the Xu language, failed to excite it to speech. Wearying at last of his pointless inquisition, Zloigm uttered the Greater Dismissal, and, obliterating the nine pentacles of Sgandrom and extinguishing the sanguinary luminance of the seven lamps of hollowed ruby, he broke at the four cardinal points the triply drawn circle of phosphoric powder, and closed his Book.

Fatigued to the extremities of his vigor by his unremitting thaumaturgical labors, the ophidian necromancer glided from the conjurational chamber and sought to recreate himself by a stroll through the gardens adjacent to his tower. This pleasaunce, however, to his surprise and consternation, he discovered no longer to exist. Instead of his topiary garden of bizarre Mesozoic flora, he found himself amidst a foetid grove of loathsome and tumescent fungi, whose swollen and phallic and hooded crests soared swaying to every side, exuding a singularly vile and noxious putrescence, even as their glistening and spongy boles were stained and blotched with the rancid cankers of oozing and liquescent decay.

Unable to easily account for this cryptic phenomenon, Zloigm traversed the fungus-grove with the boneless and undulant grace of his kind, fastidiously avoiding the slightest contact with the pustulant and sickening growths. He sought instead the peaceful shores of the bitter and lonely tarn, where it was oft his wont to stroll the crystalline strand in melancholy reverie. But the tarn, as well, had inexplicably vanished, and in its place he found himself gliding the giddy verge of a precipitous chasm. And within the depths of this abyss he glimpsed scarlet horrors of indefinite shape that writhed and slithered in the most noxiously suggestive manner amidst miasmic and bubbling slime.

It became indubitable that some malign transformation had been worked upon Zloigm's solitary demesne, doubtless through the enchantments of an insidious and vindictive rival. Turning from the lip of the shadowy gulf, wherein whose deeps the half-glimpsed horrors had not ceased from their repugnant and profoundly disquieting wrigglings, the necromancer sought again the sanctuary of his lone and solitary citadel—only to find a further encroachment of the metamorphosis, which he now saw to be progressive. For in the place of his somber and majestic tower there now rose an atrocious structure of virulent and nauseous hues, constructed according to the haphazard principals of some weird and prodigiously alien geometry. The eyewrenching colors and dizzying, impossible curves and angles of the architectural abomination were utterly repugnant to one of his race and temperament.

As he contemplated the loathsome spire with commingled bewilderment and ire, there slowly rose into view behind it an immense and dimly luminous orb of ghastly and leprous hue. Zloigm at once recognized the mottled and ebbing luminary for that wan, demising star about which the insect-sages had informed him the else-deserted world of the philosophic mould revolved. And there came to him there, as he stood amidst the festering grove of stalked and nodding fungi, some intimation of the extent of his predicament. It was not, as he had first conjectured, the malison of some iniquitous rival sorcerer which had worked this malevolent metamorphosis—*but his own temerity in uttering the forbidden and blasphemic ritual.*

Indeed, so titanic had been his efforts to force the obdurate Crxyxll hither, that he had bent awry the very fabric of space itself, and his own somber spire and the garish and atrocious abode of the alien entity now simultaneously occupied the same point in space and time. The fullest implications of this uncanny simultaneity did not at once dawn upon the cold intelligence of the ophidian: neither did he suffer undue dismay or perturbation at the *ominous tendency* of this sequence of transmutations, for he knew that the texture of space is pliable and resilient only to a degree, and that this unnatural condition could not long endure and would soon terminate, the superimposed towers returning each to its customary coign at opposite poles of the universe. As well, his memory retained spells and cantrips of prodigious and transcendent magnitude, the very utterance of which would summon to his aid, across the breadth of the cosmos itself if need be, daemons and genii and elementals of awful and terrific mightiness, bound to his servitude by unsunderable vows.

Therefore it was with a certain chill amusement than with any trepidation that he traversed the loathsome garden towards the alien spire of revolting configuration and nauseating hues, but, of a sudden, found the undulant, gliding perambulation of his serpent-kind now altered to a mode of peculiar and unseemly locomotion. In a word, he now moved forward by a singular crepitation of innumerous segmentations, and, turning his astounding vision upon his own person, he saw, by a sense of perception in no wise identical with sight, that the sequential transformation was now, presumably, complete: and that he had *himself* become interchanged with the being of the recalcitrant Crxyxll, and was now become a squirming and disgusting thing like unto a white and crawling mould.

The matrix of space and time shimmered and then grew stable again, but the alien panorama remained unchanged.

He realized by this that the innate resilience of space had, as anticipated, re-asserted itself, the unnatural simultaneity of the double tower had terminated—but that he remained trapped in this hideous travesty of a form, while, presumably, the mind and spirit of the mould-philosopher currently resided in his own superior and comely body, doubtless even at this moment sampling the elaborate spectrum of sensuous and aesthetic pleasures the unique accommodations of his tower afforded.

Even before the whelming realization, Zloigm did not deign to yield to despair: for the metamorphosed ophidian knew that to give utterance to the name of but one of the potent genii who served him would undo this dreadful and nightmarish transmutation.

He thought, therefore, to open his lipless mouth in order to cry aloud, in the hissing and sibilant speech of his kind, upon Marbas or Focalor or Zepar or Bifrons. But no outward physical manifestation accompanied the mental command. Then, and then only, did the misfortunate necromancer taste the full bitterness of despair and horror, and savor the gall of the knowledge of his peculiar doom.

For the sentient crawling white mould, whose body he now inhabited forever, quite naturally, alike all of its extinct kind, possessed no slightest vestige of the organs of audible speech.

Fritz Leiber

TRAPPED IN THE SHADOWLAND

I think Fritz Leiber is the finest living writer of heroic fantasy, and the adventures of Fafhrd and the Gray Mouser are high on any reader's list of favorite Sword & Sorcery series. Recently, Fritz has been turning out new chapters in the saga for Ted White's popular magazine, Fantastic. Here, from a recent issue, is the latest exploit of our favorite pair of rogues and rapscallions. Admittedly a minor effort, even minor Leiber is major in my estimate.

—LC

Fafhrd and the Gray Mouser were almost dead from thirst. Their horses had died from the same Hell-throated ailment at the last waterhole, which had proved dry. Even the last contents of their waterbags, augmented by water of their own bodies, had not been enough to keep alive the dear dumb equine beasts. As all men know, camels are the only creatures who can carry men for more than a day or two across the almost supernaturally hot arid deserts of the World of Nehwon.

They tramped on south-westward under the blinding sun and over the burning sand. Despite their desperate plight and heat-fevered minds and bodies, they were steering a canny course. Too far south and they would fall into the cruel hands of the emperor of the Eastern Lands, who would find rare delight in torturing them before killing them. Too far east and they would encounter the merciless Mingols of the Steppes and other horrors. West and northwest were those who were pursuing them now. While north and northeast lay the Shadowland, the home of Death himself. So much they well knew of the geography of Nehwon.

Meanwhile, Death grinned faintly in his low castle in the heart of the Shadowland, certain that he had at last got the two elusive heroes in his bony grip. They had years ago had the nerve to enter his domain, visiting their first loves, Ivrian and Vlana, and even stealing from his very castle Death's favorite mask. Now they would pay for their temerity.

Death had the appearance of a tall, handsome young man, though somewhat cadaverous and of opalescent complexion. He was staring now at a large map of the Shadowland and its environs set in a dark wall of his dwelling. On this map Fafhrd and the Mouser were a gleaming speck, like an errant star or fire beetle, south of the Shadowland.

Death writhed his thin, smiling lips and moved his bony fingertips in tiny, cabalistic curves, as he worked a small but difficult magic.

His incantation done, he noted with approval that on the map a southern tongue of the Shadowland was visibly extending itself in pursuit of the dazzling speck that was his victims.

Fafhrd and the Mouser tramped on south, staggering and reeling now, their feet and minds aflame, their faces a-drip with precious sweat. They had been seeking, near the Sea of Monsters and the City of Ghouls, their strayed newest girls, Mouser's Reetha and Fafhrd's Kreeshkra, the latter a Ghoul herself, all her blood and flesh invisible, which made her bonny pink bones stand out the more, while Reetha believed in going naked and shaven from head to toe, a taste which gave the girls a mutual similarity and sympathy.

But the Mouser and Fafhrd had found nothing but a horde of fierce male Ghouls, mounted on equally skeletal horses, who had chased them east and south, either to slay them, or to cause them to die of thirst in the desert or of torture in the dungeons of the King of Kings.

It was high noon and the sun was hottest. Fafhrd's left hand touched in the dry heat a cool fence about two feet high, invisible at first though not for long.

"Escape to damp coolth," he said in a cracked voice. They eagerly clambered over the fence and threw themselves down on a blessed thick turf of dark grass two inches high, over which a fine mist was falling. They slept about ten hours.

In his castle Death permitted himself a thin grin, as on his map the south-trending tongue of the Shadowland touched the diamond spark and dimmed it.

Nehwon's greatest star, Astorian, was mounting the eastern sky, precursor of the moon, as the two adventurers awoke, greatly refreshed by their long nap. The mist had almost ceased, but the only star visible was vast Astorian.

The Mouser sprang up agitatedly in his gray hood, tunic, and ratskin shoes. "We must escape backward to hot dryth," he said, "for this is the Shadowland, Death's homeland."

"A very comfortable place," Fafhrd replied, stretching his huge muscles luxuriously on the thick greensward. "Return to the briny, granular, rasping, fiery land-sea? Not I."

"But if we stay here," the Mouser countered, "we will be will-lessly drawn by devilish and delusive will-o-the-wisps to the low-walled Castle of Death, whom we defied by stealing his mask and giving its two halves to our wizards Sheelba and Ningauble, an action for which Death is not likely to love us. Besides, here we might well meet our two first girls, Ivrian and Vlana, now concubines of Death, and that would not be a pleasant experience."

Fafhrd winced, yet stubbornly repeated, "But it is comfortable here." Rather self-consciously he writhed his great shoulders and restretched his seven feet on the deliciously damp turf. (The "seven feet" refers to his height. He was by no means an octopus missing one limb, but a handsome, red-bearded, very tall barbarian.)

The Mouser persisted, "But what *if* your Vlana should

appear, blue-faced and unloving? Or my Ivrian in like state, for that matter?"

That dire image did it. Fafhrd sprang up, grabbing for the low fence. But—lo and behold—there was no fence at hand. In all directions stretched out the damp, dark green turf of the Shadowland, while the soft drizzle had thickened again, hiding Astorian. There was no way to tell directions.

The Mouser searched in his ratskin pouch and drew out a blue bone needle. He pricked himself finding it, and cursed. It was wickedly sharp at one end, round and pierced at the other.

"We need a pool or puddle," he said.

"Where did you get that toy?" Fafhrd quizzed. "Magic, eh?"

"From Nattick Nimblefingers the Tailor in vasty Lankhmar," the Mouser responded. "Magic, nay! Hast heard of compass needles, oh wise one?"

Not far off they found a shallow puddle atop the turf. The Mouser carefully floated his needle on the small mirror of clear, placid water. It spun about slowly and eventually settled itself.

"We go that way," Fafhrd said, pointing out from the pierced end of the needle. "South." For he realized the pricking end must point toward the heart of the Shadowland—Nehwon's Death Pole, one might call it. For an instant he wondered if there were another such pole at the antipodes—perhaps a Life Pole.

"And we'll still need the needle," the Mouser added, pricking himself again and cursing as he pouched it, "for future guidance."

"Hah! Wah-wah-wah-*hah!*" yelled three berserks, emerging like fleet statues from the mist. They had been long marooned in the skirts of the Shadowland, reluctant either to advance to the Castle of Death and find their Hell or Valhalla, or to seek escape, but always ready for a fight. They rushed at Fafhrd and the Mouser, bareskinned and naked-bladed.

It took the Twain ten heartbeats of clashing swordfight to kill them, though killing in the domain of Death must be at least a misdemeanor, it occurred to the Mouser—like poaching. Fafhrd got a shallow slash wound across his biceps, which the Mouser carefully bound up.

"Wow!" said Fafhrd. "Where did the needle point? I've got turned around."

They located the same or another puddle-mirror, floated the needle, again found South, and then took up their trek.

They twice tried to escape from the Shadowland by changing course, once east, once west. It was no use. Whatever way they went, they found only soft-turfed earth and bemisted sky. So they kept on south, trusting Nattick's needle.

For food they cut out black lambs from the black flocks they encountered, slew, bled, skinned, dressed, and roasted the tender meat over fires from wood of the squat black trees and bushes here and there. The young flesh was succulent. They drank dew.

Death in his low-walled keep continued to grin from time to time at his map, as the dark tongue of his territory kept magically extending southwest, the dimmed spark of his doomed victims in its margin.

He noted that the Ghoulish cavalry originally pursuing the Twain had halted at the boundary of his marchland.

But now there was the faintest trace of anxiety in Death's smile. And now and again a tiny vertical frown creased his opalescent, unwrinkled forehead, as he exerted his faculties to keep his geographical sorcery going.

The black tongue kept on down the map, past Sarheenmar and thievish Ilthmar to the Sinking Land. Both cities on the shore of the Inner Sea were scared unto death by the dark invasion of damp turf and misty sky, and they thanked their degenerate gods that it narrowly bypassed them.

And now the black tongue crossed the Sinking Land, moving due west. The little frown in Death's forehead had become quite deep. At the Swamp Gate of Lankhmar the Mouser and Fafhrd found their magical mentors waiting, Sheelba of the Eyeless Face and Ningauble of the Seven Eyes.

"What have you been up to?" Sheelba sternly asked the Mouser.

"And what have *you* been doing?" Ningauble demanded of Fafhrd.

The Mouser and Fafhrd were still in the Shadowland, and the two wizards outside it, with the boundary midway between. So their conversation was like that of two pairs of people on opposite sides of a narrow street, on the one side of which it is raining cats and dogs, the other side dry and sunny, though in this instance stinking with the smog of Lankhmar.

"Seeking Reetha," the Mouser replied, honestly for once.

"Seeking Kreeshkra," Fafhrd said boldly, "but a mounted Ghoul troop harried us back."

From his hood Ningauble writhed out six of his seven eyes and regarded Fafhrd searchingly. He said severely, "Kreeshkra, tired of your untameable waywardness, has gone back to the Ghouls for good, taking Reetha with her. I would advise you instead to seek Frix," naming a remarkable female who had played no small part in the adventure of the rat-hordes, the same affair in which Kreeshkra the Ghoul girl had been involved.

"I have heard that Frix is a brave and handsome woman," Fafhrd temporized, "but how to reach her? She's in another world, if what I have been told be true."

"While I counsel that *you* seek Hisvet," Sheelba of the Eyeless Face told the Mouser grimly. The unfeatured blackness in *his* hood grew yet blacker (with concentration) if that were possible. He was referring to yet another female involved in the rat-adventure, in which Reetha also had been a leading character.

"A great idea, Father," responded the Mouser, who made no bones about preferring Hisvet to all other girls, particularly since he had never once enjoyed her favors, though on the verge of doing so several times. "But she is likely deep in the earth and in her rat-size persona. How would I do it? How, how?"

If Sheel and Ning could have smiled, they would have.

However, Sheelba said only, "It is bothersome to see you both bemisted, like heroes in smoke."

He and Ning, without conference, collaborated in working a small but very difficult magic. After resisting most tenaciously, the Shadowland and its drizzle retreated east, leaving the Twain in the same sunshine as their mentors. Though two invisible patches of dark mist remained, entering into the flesh of the Mouser and Fafhrd and closing forever around their hearts.

Far eastaways, Death permitted himself a small curse

which would have scandalized the high gods, had they heard it. He looked daggers at his map and its shortening black tongue. For Death, he was in a most bitter temper. Foiled again!

Ning and Sheel worked another diminutive wizardry.

Without warning, Fafhrd shot upwards in the air, growing tinier and tinier, until at last he was lost to sight.

Without moving from where he stood, the Mouser also grew tiny, until he was somewhat less than a foot high, of a size to cope with Hisvet, in or out of bed. He dove into the nearest rathole.

Neither feat was as remarkable as it sounds, since Nehwon is only a bubble rising through the waters of infinity.

The two heroes each spent a delightful weekend with his lady of the week.

"I don't know why I do things like this," Hisvet said, lisping faintly and touching the Mouser intimately as they lay side by side supine on silken sheets. "It must be because I loathe you."

"A pleasant and even worthy encounter," Frix confessed to Fafhrd in similar situation. "It is my hang-up to enjoy playing, now and then, with the lower animals. Which some would say is a weakness in a queen of the air."

Their weekend done, Fafhrd and the Mouser were automatically magicked back to Lankhmar, encountering one another in Cheap Street near Nattick Nimblefinger's narrow and dirty-looking dwelling. The Mouser was his right size again.

"You look sunburned," he observed to his comrade.

"Space-burned, it is," Fafhrd corrected. "Frix lives in a remarkably distant land. But you, old friend, look paler than your wont."

"Shows what three days underground will do to a man's complexion," the Mouser responded. "Come, let's have a drink at the Silver Eel."

Ningauble in his cave near Ilthmar and Sheelba in his mobile hut in the Great Salt Marsh each smiled, though lacking the equipment for that facial expression. They knew they had laid one more obligation on their protegés.

Lin Carter

BLACK HAWK OF VALKARTH

> *Ted White's magazine has also offered a new home to the adventures of my own Sword & Sorcery character, Thongor the Mighty, warrior-hero of Lost Lemuria, whose saga I have been writing now for ten years. This new story, however, is quite recent and may be of interest to those readers who only know Thongor from his novel-length adventures —for this is the first of all the Thongor stories, the very first chapter in his saga—the "origin story," if you will. I hope it meets with your approval.*

> —LC

CHAPTER 1.

Blood on the Snow

The flames of sunset died to glowing coals in the crimson west. Slowly, the brooding skies darkened overhead, and the first few stars glared down upon a scene of terrible carnage.

It was a great valley in the land of Valkarth in the Northlands, beyond the mountains of Mommur, where the cold black waves of Zharanga Tethrabaal the Great North Ocean lashed a bleak and rock-strewn coast.

63

Although it was late spring, snow lay thick upon the valley. It was trampled and torn, and here and there bestrewn with motionless black shapes. These were the bodies of men and women and children, clad in furs and leathern harness, clasping broken weapons in stiff, dead hands. In their hundreds they lay sprawled and scattered amid the trampled snow, and against its dirty grey their blood was crimson.

The battle had begun at the birth of the day and with day's end it, too, had ended. All the long, weary day the warriors and hunters and chieftains of the Black Hawk nation had stood knee-deep in the snows and fought with iron blade and wooden club and stone axe against the enemies that had crept upon them in the night. One by one they had fallen, and now no single man lived or moved upon the gore-drenched snows of Valkarth. They had not died easily, but they had died; and very many of their foes lay beside them in the black sleep of death.

The valley was like a charnel-pit. And the stars looked down, wonderingly.

They had been a mighty people. The men were tall, strongthewed, with thick black manes and virile, golden eyes. The women were deep-breasted, their unshorn hair worn in heavy braids, their strong white bodies clad in belted furs against the bite of wintry winds. They had fought beside their men, the women of the Black Hawk clan, or back-to-back, and they too had heaped their dead before them. In the end they had gone down fighting; and their young, too, children scarce old enough to walk, had died with bloody knives clenched in their small fists.

Life in the bleak Northlands of lost Lemuria was one unending struggle against grim Nature, ferocious beasts, and no less savage men. The weaklings and the cowards die young: this nation had been strong, and it had died hard; but in the end it had died.

By one great rock a tall and stalwart warrior had taken his last stand. He had set his back against that rock and with his great sword he had hewn and hewn until the snowy slope before him was buried beneath the corpses of those who had come up against him. They had cut him down with arrows at the last, no longer daring to come within the reach of that terrible blade; at that, it had taken five arrows to kill him. He lay now with his broad shoulders still flat against the rock, his square-jawed face grim in death as in life, snow and blood bedabbled on his thick grey mane and beard. The wife of his youth lay beside him, a bear-spear still held in her cold hands, her head resting lightly against his shoulder. They had cut her down with an axe, and two of her tall sons and her young daughter lay near.

The name of the dead warrior had been Thumithar; he had been a chieftain of the clan, of direct descent in the male line from the hero Valkh—Valkh the Black Hawk, Valkh of Nemedis, the seventh of the sons of Thungarth of the first Kingdoms of Man. The war bards of the tribe, the old, fierce-eyed sagamen, told it had been Valkh who had founded the Black Hawk nation in time's grey dawn. And the great broadsword that lay still clasped in the dead fingers of Thumithar was none other than Sarkozan itself, the very Sword of Valkh.

He had been a wise chieftain, had Thumithar, just and strong. And a great war-leader, and a mighty hunter.

He would hunt no more, would Thumithar, with his tall sons at his side.

In that grim panorama of death, one indeed yet lives. He was a scrawny boy, scarce fifteen, naked save for a ragged clout and a cloak of furs slung about bare shoulders. They were broad, those shoulders, but stooped with weariness now, and they bore a burden of sorrow, heavy for one so young to bear.

Blood was bright on the brown hide of his deep chest, and some of it was the blood of the foemen he had fought and slain, but much of it was his own. He limped through the bloody snow, dragging one foot behind him, and, now again, he paused to look at this dead face and that one. He knew many of them, the dead faces; but he did not find the one he was looking for.

At last he came up to the place where the grey-maned warrior had taken his last stand, and the limping boy flinched at the sight of that dead face in the starlight. And the serene face of the woman that lay beside the dead man wrung a sharp cry from the white lips of the boy.

He crumpled into the snow before them on his knees and he hid his face in his hands. Tears leaked slowly through the blood-crusted fingers, and he wept there at last—he who had not wept before.

His name was Thongor.

CHAPTER 2.

The Cairn in the Valley

After a time the boy climbed wearily to his feet and stood staring at the ruin of his world. In repose, he had the same grim-jawed face as his father, the same heavy, unshorn mane—save his was yet untouched with grey. His eyes glared golden like the eyes of lions, under scowling black brows. He had long, rangy legs, and strong arms seamed with scars, some of which were raw wounds.

In the crush and swirl of battle, he had been swept away from his father and his mother and his brothers. All day he had fought alone, with the tigerish fury of a young berserker, and many of the enemy had fallen before his murderous wrath. When his old sword broke in his hands, he had fought on with the stub, then with rocks clawed up from the snowy ground—finally, with his bare fingers and his strong white teeth.

He had taken a deep wound on the breast, and lesser wounds on thigh and shoulder and brow. He was splattered with blood from head to foot, although he had staunched the bleeding with snow until the wounds were numb.

The Snow Bear warriors had clubbed him down and beaten him to earth and left him for dead. That was their only mistake.

For he had not died.

He had slowly climbed back from the Shadowlands into the realm of the living again, to find night fallen and the battle over and the terrible valley silent with its dead. Slowly, dragging his injured foot behind him, he had searched among the fallen until at last he had found that which he sought. And now he knew what he must do.

He cleared away a patch of earth, clawing back the snow, and he laid out the bodies of his mother and father beside the bodies of his older brothers and his younger sister.

He set their weapons beside them. All but the great sword of his father, the mighty broadsword Sarkozan; that he took, for he would need it.

He kissed their cold lips one last time in farewell.

Then he began to pile the stones upon them.

There must be many stones, else the beasts would feed upon them in the night. Although he was bone-weary, and sick with loss of blood, he dragged the great stones one by one upon them, heaping up a tall cairn until it stood higher than a grown man. Then, and then only, did he rest; and by then he was shaking with exhaustion.

It would stand for the rest of time, that cairn, to mark the place where Thumithar of the Valklings had fallen. Or until the mighty continent itself, riven asunder with earthquake, was drowned beneath the cold waves of the sea.

He sang the warrior's song over them, his clear young voice sharp and strong and strange to hear in that deathly silence.

The black sky lit with cold glory as the great golden Moon of old Lemuria rose up over the edges of the world to flood the bleak land of Valkarth with her light.

In the cold flame of the moonlight, he saw that the cairn was high and strong. The white bears would not claw it asunder, nor the grey wolves, to feast of what lay beneath.

At the thought, his jaws tightened and his lips clamped together. For the white bear of the Northlands was the totem beast of the enemy clan who had worked this day's red ruin, even as the black hawk of the skies was his own tribal totem.

He hated the mighty *ulth*, the white bear of the snow countries, and had oft hunted him down the bleak hills of this wintry land. And now he had another reason for that hatred.

The cairn was done; and he was finished here.

But there was one last task the dead had set upon him.

And its name was Vengeance.

CHAPTER 3.

Demon of the Snows

He gathered up his gear and was ready to depart. From the dead, he took what he needed, nor did it bother him to plunder them. They were the men of his race, and the blood that lay strewn upon the snows about them, that same blood ran hot and fierce in his own veins. They would not begrudge him what he needed of them. Nor would they need it any longer.

From one he took the black leathern trappings that were warriors' harness, the leathern yoke studded with discs of brass that fitted about the throat to protect the shoulders, the affair of buckled straps and the great brass ring that shielded the midsection from the flat of a blade, the iron-studded girdle worn low about the hips, the heavy boots, the broad-bladed dagger and the twin leathern bottles, one filled with water and one with wine. His sword he slid into its worn old scabbard, which he clipped to a baldric and slung it across his chest so that the scabbard hung high between his shoulders.

He was not truly of age to don warriors' harness, for he had not yet undergone initiation into the rites of manhood by the old shaman of his nation. Nor would he now, for the garrulous old tosspot lay dead across the vale, having slain a dozen Snow Bear warriors with a two-handed axe before they cut him down. Had not this day befallen, he would with summer have gone up into the high mountains, there to dwell alone amid the heights, drinking the water of melted snow and eating only what he could slay with his bare hands; there would he have dwelt for forty days until the vision of his totem came to him and he learned his secret name.

Now that would never be. But manhood was upon him without the old rites.

Vengeance is for men. It is not a task for boys.

Half the night was worn away. He crossed the valley and climbed the hills, ignoring the pain in his injured foot. Strong red wine had warmed his numb flesh and it drove new strength and vigor through his tired frame. The cold, thin air of the heights cleared his throbbing head and the exertion of the ascent made the blood tingle in his veins.

There would be time enough to rest, later, when the deed was done.

If he lived . . .

The Moon was high in the heavens now; the night sky was black as death and the stars blazed like diamonds strewn on dark velvet. He thought of nothing as he climbed, neither of the dead he had left behind him in the valley, nor of those he went to kill, but merely of setting his foot upon first one rock and then upon a higher one until at last he came to the crest and the wide world fell away beneath him to every side and the stars seemed very near.

Here a saddle-shaped depression sloped between twin hillcrests, thick with virgin snow. It had fallen here, mayhap, when the world was young and fresh and the Gods still went among men to teach them the nine crafts and the seven arts.

He began to wade through the snow between the twin peaks. With each step he stirred snows that had lain for a thousand years, and the crystals swirled up before him like ancient ghosts awakened by the step of a rash intruder into places better left undisturbed.

His nape-hairs prickled and the flesh of his forearms crept. He had a sense that something was aware of his coming, that something—*roused*.

The cold breath of fear blew along his nerves, and it was colder than any snow. One hand went to his breast where a fetish of white stone lay over his heart, suspended about his neck on a thong. He muttered aloud the name of Gorm, his god.

And terror woke, roaring!

Was it a sudden gust of wind which raised the snow before him in a whirling cloud—a cloud that shaped itself into a mighty, towering form—a phantom-thing of numb snow that reared up before him on legs like tree-trunks, hunched shoulders massive and monstrous, huge paws raised to crush and tear, dripping jaws agape, red eyes of madness glaring into his?

He fell into a fighting stance and the great blade was alive and singing in his hand, starlight glittering on the blue steel, acid-etched sigils blazing with eerie fires.

The thing came lumbering towards him. And he knew no steel could slay it, for it did not really live.

CHAPTER 4.

Vengeance in the Night

The gigantic, white, hulking monster was almost upon the boy now. He knew it for an *ulth*, a snow bear, but twice the girth and height of any *ulth* ever seen by mortal eyes before.

He knew also that it was a ghost-thing, that demon of the snows. For there poured from it a freezing cold, inhuman and magical. The sheen of perspiration on his bronze limbs froze like a thin sheath of glass upon his body. The icy breath of those fanged jaws panted in his face and he felt his face go dead and numb as if he wore a mask of snow.

A red haze thickened before his eyes, blinding him. Each breath he drew was like fire stabbing in his lungs, cold fire, black yet burning. He fought against the cold that coiled about him, swung Sarkozan high, glittering against the stars, and hewed and cut at the ghost-bear. But from each stroke he took hurt, for a wave of stunning cold went through him as the steel blade touched the lumbering monster of snow.

He fought on, knowing death was near; flesh could not long endure such cold. His heart was a frozen thing in his breast; his very blood congealed in his veins; he could no longer breathe, for to draw in each breath was as painful as a blade of ice driven deep into his lungs. But he fought on, and would fight until he fell.

A piercing cry cut through him from above.

Through snow-thick lashes he peered up to see a weird and fantastic shape, black and bewinged, beating against the stars.

He could not see it clearly—a moving blackness, blotting out the starlight—its eyes like golden fire, brighter than any star, and moonlight glittering on beak and out-stretched claws.

It fell like a thunderbolt from above, swept by him like a whirlwind, and swung down upon the white bear-thing with a scream of fury.

The mountains shook as the two came together, and the stars were blotted out.

Ragged black wings beat with cyclone force. Shaggy white jaws roared and crunched. Scythe-sharp black claws caught at the white breast and tore it asunder. The white thing moaned, and toppled, and came apart in chunks of broken snow.

The black shape whirled about and glared at the boy for the space of a single heart-beat.

And eyes of burning gold blazed deep into golden eyes.

Then the black wings spread and caught the wind and it was gone and Thongor lay gasping in the snow, the sword fallen from his nerveless hand.

Agony lanced through him as circulation returned to his half-frozen body. Hot blood went pumping through numb flesh; he shook his head dully, trying to waken his sluggish, frozen brain.

He had attained manhood, after all.

He had gone up on the heights alone, and there the vision had come to him, and he had seen his totem-beast, and learned his True Name.

And he was blest above all the warriors of his tribe since time began: for the beast of his vision was the Black Hawk of Valkarth itself, the symbol of his race. And he knew then that his destiny would be stranger and more wondrous and more terrible than that of oth-er men.

And he had seen a prophecy, too.

He had seen the Black Hawk fight and slay the Snow Bear. The ghost-beasts had fought there on the windy heights near to the blazing stars, and from that fight the Black Hawk had borne away the victory.

He drank down cold wine, and rested for a time.

Then he went on, to make the prophecy come true.

It was the month of Garang in late spring, and the thaws had begun. The great snows that lay thick upon the heights and that cumbered the steep slope of the cliffs was rotten and lay loose, water trickling here and there. When he crossed over to the other side of the ridge he could look down on the valley where the tents of the Snow Bear tribe stood black against the snow, which reddened, now, to the first shafts of dawn.

They were weary after the long battle, the Snow Bear warriors—those of them that had survived. They had killed and killed and come away with the Black Hawk treasure of mammoth-ivory and red gold and with those of the Black Hawk women and girl-children who had not been fortunate enough to die beside their men.

They had feasted long, drunk deep, and caroused lustily and late, the victorious Snow Bear warriors. And now they slept heavily, gorged on meat and blood and wine and womanflesh.

From that sleep they would not awaken.

For a long moment the boy stood, arms folded against his breast, looking down on the camp.

His face was grim and expressionless, like a mask cast in hard bronze. He was a boy in years, but the iron of manhood had entered his soul. He knew what he must do; the spirits of the dead called to him in the windy silence, and he hearkened, and bent to the task.

With the great sword he began to cut the snow away.

It was not hard to do; the growing warmth of a Northlands spring had done half the job for him. The broken masses of snow began to roll down the steep, high slopes; as they came whirling down, they broke more snow loose, and each mass became a greater mass, until at last a mountain of heavy snow poured like a ponderous white river down the cliffs to collide in thunder on the floor of the valley below.

They had put up their tents close under the cliffs, the Snow Bear warriors, to block away the wind. Now it was snow that came down upon them, not wind, and by the time the avalanche came thundering down upon the tents it weighed many tons.

It crushed them into the earth, smothered them and their treasure and the ruined, broken, empty-eyed women they had taken captive; and in that thundering white fury not one lived.

The tribes of Valkarth have a simple faith.

Only those brave warriors who face the foe, and fight, and fall in battle, only their bold spirits are borne by the War Maids to the Hall of Heroes, to feast eternity away before the throne of Father Gorm.

And what of they that die by accident in gross and drunken slumber? The shamans shrug and do not say. But they did not die the death of men, the death of warriors; the Hall of Heroes does not ope to such as they. Their miserable souls slink cringing through the grey mists and cold shadows of the Underworld forever.

The vengeance of Thongor was completed.

CHAPTER 5.

Red Dawn

Morning lit the east and the stars fled, one by one, before the red shafts of dawn.

When Thongor had made certain that not a single foe survived the avalanche, he turned away and set his face to the sun.

The task was accomplished, and he had lived.

Where, now, would he go? To a valley of corpses and an empty hut, whose walls would ring no more to his father's joyous laughter and his mother's quiet, crooning songs?

Not there; he could not go back.

But where, then? No other tribe would take him in, for life in the Northlands was a grim, bleak struggle for existence, and every mouth that is fed means that another must go hungry.

His people were extinct; there was nowhere for him to go.

And then it was that a verse from the old warriors' song he had sung over his father's grave for a dirge returned to him. And he bethought him of the Southlands, of the Dakshina, the lush jungle-countries that lay beside the warm waters of the Gulf, beyond the Mountains of Mommur to the south.

There, bright young cities glittered in the bold sun, with green gardens, and laughing girls. There, fiery kings and princes contended in mighty wars, and kingdoms lay ripe and ready for the taking. He thought of gold and gems, of fruit warm from the sun, of whirling battles on the green plains, of darkeyed, barbaric women . . .

And he set the great broad sword back in its scabbard, and drank deep of the red wine, watching dawn rise up over the edges of the world to fill the land with light; and he set his face towards the south, that last of the Black Hawk warriors.

And he passed from sight, down the hill-slope, striding with long steps towards the place where the great range of purple mountains marched across the world from west to east.

His heart lifted within him, for the night was over. And as he strode from view, he lifted his voice and sang again that warriors' song . . . .

> *Out there, beyond the setting*
> *Sun,*
> *Are kingdoms waiting to be won!*
> *And crowns, and women, gold*
> *and wine—*
> *Courage! And hold the battleline!*

Hannes Bok

JEWEL QUEST

The late Hannes Bok may yet be remembered as much for his fantasy fiction as for his brilliant and beautiful drawings and paintings in the genre. His two major novels, SORCEROR'S SHIP and BEYOND THE GOLDEN STAIR, show his talents in the Merrittesque lost race story. This tale, recently discovered in manuscript, displays his gifts in a very different direction. The sly drollery and tongue-in-cheek, playful good humor evident in the story which follows are characteristic of the Hannes Bok we who knew him personally remember best. This is the first of five newly discovered stories to be published.

—LC

The golden sun sank langorously on its blue couch of the horizon, and perfumed breezes swooned through the aureate rays, caressing the lean hard yellow cheek of the Emperor Po Ko, stirring the peacock plumes of the fan which he carelessly waved in one set of lacquered claws. The Emperor was seated on his Wednesday throne of silver and malachite on the topmost terrace of his garden. He was a long thin man, like a carving in yellow icicle, and his bright blue robe, lusciously embroidered with mating dragons and flames, hung loosely about him in luxurious folds.

Beside the Emperor, on a gold-cloth cushion, sat Princess Pei Wei, Sweet Flower of Innocence that blooms

75

on the shores of scarlet lakes of dreamland when the moon is high above the white towered peaks of Ku Chu, land of mystery and ever-brooding sadness, where no storks fly except at sundown. She was a dainty little creature, like an animate flower, all tender curves and voluptuous rondures, like a Tchi Tchi nut when it bursts its amber covering and drops ripely succulent to the ground. Her pallid pink robes only accentuated the delicacy and satiny texture of her milk white skin. Her deep brown eyes languished wistfully on the face of the sovereign, who was well aware of her imploring scrutiny, but callously ignored it. He was condescending to converse with the Most High Lord Glagla, his vizier.

"Ah, despicable rodent which burrows in a pig's entrails," he said, smiling thinly and airily waving one set of fingernails at the crouching huddle which was the Vizier. "It is in our most glorious thought to undertake a pilgrimage."

"Ah," said the Vizier, "to the tomb of your illustrious ancestors, I trust, there to take counsel with your forefathers?

The Emperor tossed his head, almost shaking off his satin bonnet in his vehemence. "No, worm that we would not deign to crush beneath an unwary footstep," he sneered, just to display his diamond-studded teeth, "I am not thinking of honoring my dead relatives with my living presence. I am going to the Valley of the Fourteen Thousand Ill-Fed Vultures, there to speak the ancient charm and open the portals to Kur'czu and wrest the Jewel of Power from the Magician who resides there."

As he spoke, his eyes rested covertly on the wan face of the Princess Pei Wei, who had shuddered at his words. She lifted a dainty little palm as though about to plead with him—but a stern shake of his head silenced her. The little Princess squirmed uncomfortably upon her plump cushions, for one of her silver brooches had come unfastened; and also because she adored the Emperor with all her tender little heart.

The Vizier uncrouched, revealing himself as a toadlike old man with a crescent moon of black mustache and sharp little eyes that were like those of a boar. "Oh, do not venture into that dreadful valley, Sublimity! Some evil is certain to befall you, and already your people grumble among themselves like a stomach that has fed too well. They hint that you squander the taxes which you wring from them, and they whisper of revolt."

The Emperor negligently plucked a plume from his fan, looked it over, shrugged, and let it fall. "The snails gathered to revolt against their Lord, the Elephant, but all they got for their pains was a cessation of those pains —if you know what We mean."

Little Pei Wei spoke, her tones like flying drops of water colliding with a moonbeam-strung harp, "Oh, my Lord, do not venture alone into the Valley of the Fourteen Thousand Ill-Fed Vultures! Do not, I pray you! I love you from the depth of my bosom (shallow though it may be), and if you were to go from my side, I should pine away!"

"Hmph," said the Emperor just a shade too coldly, "I would have to be gone very long for that to occur, and since my quest will only take a week, there is no danger of pining . . ."

The Vizier's stubby fingers twisted his mustache into a pretzel. "But, O Master of my body and soul (not to mention those of my thousand ancestors), what do you plan to do in that dread place?"

The Emperor waited a full minute before replying, just to show his displeasure. "I have read in the scrolls of the scholar Wak Kee that whosoever speaks the Words of Power and enters the realm of the Magician can seize the Jewel and subjugate all men in its zone of influence. I shall carry off the Jewel, bring it here, and increase my taxes. I need a new throne for Leap-year day."

Pei Wei threw up her hands in woe. "Mighty One, I will not let you depart from me!" She scrambled up with little fluttering sighs and knelt beside him, her fragile little fingers, like five tiny honey rolls, sweetly lingering on the splendor of his robe. "Say that I may go with you! Am I not beautiful? Have you not sipped the nectar of my kisses as a butterfly drains the rose? Look upon the full moon of my face, the jade pools of my eyes! Tell me, am I not to accompany you?"

The Vizier jerked up one shoulder. The Emperor noted it, and grunted: "After all, we have been together for a month of Sundays—even if only on the Sundays—and I feel a certain affection toward you, as I feel for the sun-lit blossom withering at the close of day. Yes, you may go."

Quivering with pleasure, the Princess sank back on her cushion, her face transcendant with bliss. She spoke no more, but the Vizier argued: "Have you not read in the writings of that the Magician turns every intruder into his realm into a statue of stone? Would you dare so dire a fate?"

The Emperor sprang up and paced back and forth across the blue-glazed tiles of the parapet. "Do you think We are afraid of any paltry wizard who has not the wits to use his own magic Jewel? We are a very tiger of strength, a lion of courage, and a serpent of cunning. We leave at dawn tomorrow. And you, O my faithful Glagla, will remain behind to conduct our affairs."

The Vizier bowed three times, touching his forehead to the floor. He arose, wiping off the dust, and backed down the stairway from the terrace.

In the pale starlight which preceeded an anemic dawn, the procession of the Emperor Po Ko wound from the glittering square towers and the white blank faces of the palaces of the Imperial City of Oa, which means "river-bed once visited by the Goddess Kow Tow and her retinue of nine-hundred-and-four virtuous maidens." It was a colorful cavalcade, even in the blue half-light, for at the head of it, on bull elephants, rode a thousand steel-cuirassed warriors with long bright spears like thorns of frost. Behind them came the Imperial orchestra, three men abreast, beating drums, gongs, clashing cymbals and tinkling on crystal bells, then flute-players blowing trumpets, and lastly, thirty exquisite maidens striking babbling glissandoes on their *sarawaks*.

Then came dancers in all the flamboyancy of the rainbow reflected in a rippling pool, their gaudy scarves whirling in cloud-play as they tossed their arms. Next, bedecked with plumes, came the Emperor's palanquin, in which, on cushions like juicy ripe plums, rode the Emperor's cat.

The Emperor modestly bestrode a shaggy Bactrian camel, clad in somber brown. The camel, that is; the Emperor wore scarlet. Behind him the beautiful Pei Wei indolently reclined upon a litter borne by snow-white bulls. If she wore anything, it is not recorded. Guards brought up the rear of this procession.

Slowly the magnificent equipage wended across the dusty plain to the sheer precipices of the road from the Emperor's city. A cold breeze lurched down upon the wayfarers, whispering huskily of dire misfortune lying in wait.

At last, just before sunrise, the travelers halted on the heights above the Valley of the Fourteen Thousand Ill-Fed Vultures. It was as weird a sight as ever shocked the eye of any timorous wanderer. Far below the valley lay like a cracked and smoke-fouled cup, bestrewn with what seemed to be gigantic skulls barren of all flesh for who knows how many uncounted ages. And white serpents of incredible size oozed through one eye and out between the jaws of these skulls, till it looked as if the fleshless mouths were uttering ectoplasmic sentences. Then, as the sun slunk upward, the intensifying light disclosed that the skulls were actually white meteorites and the serpents merely tendrils of vagrant mist.

"Down!" the Emperor shouted, pointing majestically, and urging his camel along with a refined jab from his spurs. But the others hung back, immobile with dread, and only little Pei Wei and her fifty snow-white bulls dared follow him. Down they went, down the winding little track that mocked any suggestion of a road, their figures dwindling with distance until they were like two sparks of flame in a heap of embers.

Po Ko halted his camel and leaped lightly to the ground, as lightly as a star petal flickering down to the calm mirror of a shallow pool. Pei Wei gave him her hand and he kissed and then assisted her down from the litter.

There they stood, the two of them, alone in the valley with fifty bulls and a single Bactrian camel, before the greatest of the meteorites. Then the Emperor raised his arms with a backward look to see how his retinue on the rim of the valley was taking it, and shouted in stentorian tones: "Open, realm of the dread sorcerer Chen yu!"

For a moment—a long moment of dark foreboding—there was an ominous silence, broken only by the echoes of the Emperor's challenge. Then from deep underground there rolled a raucous thundering. From those above who watched—all that glittering assemblage—dropped a shriek of terror. The meteorite trembled with the violence of the crescendent sound. It split, and up from the cleft flew a dark cloud of wheeling vultures, their black wings whirring, making a wind that stirred the dust of the valley and blotted out the sun.

The Emperor stood his ground, but Pei Wei trembled, in a well-bred manner, and hurried to him, her soft hands clutching his garment. "Oh, my Lord!" she wailed. "Oh, my Ancestors!" he replied. But he would not budge, though the whirling vultures swooped menacingly, clicking their beaks—all fourteen thousand of them. The watchers above reiterated their screams of despair, and as one man (though there were women present) they turned and fled in a stampede of camels, elephants, horses, scarves, flute players, and the Emperor's cat. They vanished from view in a trice.

The cloud of vultures dispersed, and the meteorite fell apart, disclosing a black stairway leading down into the very bowels of the earth (whence came the muffled rumbling). Pei Wei peered into the opening timorously, but Po Ko did not hold back. Squaring his shoulders manfully, he strode forward. Pei Wei shivered, but she crept after him. It was dark within the meteorite, but there was a faint glimmering of light ahead of them. Shadows were everywhere. In the gloom they could not see. The Stygian atmosphere was quite appalling; it was as if they had been born sightless, or there had never been a sun.

Slowly the mote of dim light ahead of them brightened as the stair ended and they stooped through a low tunnel. Now they could see the light was a doorway, but a very small one. "Goodness," sighed Pei Wei, "however am I going to wedge through that?"

"Big boats have coursed small canals," her companion said sagely. "Yes," she replied sweetly, "but the swan does not sit in the sparrow's nest." "Even the rose closes its lovely lips in the darkness," Po Ko snapped. "Ah, but only in the murky sea are pearls born," she chimed; but she got the point.

When they reached the doorway, it was not as tiny as it seemed and dainty Pei Wei had no difficulty in squeezing through. They stood in an immense cavern whose sides dripped veils of lacy water, illuminated by the glare of artificial suns. Ahead of them loomed the golden dome of Chen yu's palace, like a bubble of gilded glass floating on a sheet of quicksilver.

They started forward, Pei Wei trembling at the strangeness of it all, Po Ko brazen and fearless. Then the waterfall to their left parted as though it were a portiere of crystal beads, and out of it stepped a small bent figure, like an imitation shadow executed in dirty cobwebs. It hovered there for a moment, regarding them, then casually stepped to the cavern floor and preceded them. It raised its hand in a magic gesture, and on every side, the waterfalls no longer rained. As if they had been unveiled for a public dedication, statues stood disclosed —human-sized statues, cubistic and deformed, but still recognizable as having once been men, or animals, or birds or even fish. They had gems for eyes, and the facets glinted in the hard brilliant light as if they were alive and winking. Pei Wei was so frightened that she screamed, choked, gasped, strangled, and fell down in a dead faint. Po Ko wondered whether it was a faint or a feint. But he did not need her at the moment, and she would be safe here if he were to go and steal the jewel. So he strode onward.

But at her cry, the Magician's little dark shape turned. Chen yu hurried back to the unconscious girl and bent over her. The Emperor halted uneasily and watched as Chen yu stroked her sleek dark hair, so like black lacquer, with his crooked hand, incidentally removing her diamond ornaments as he did so, which he thrust beneath his cloak. Then he lifted the dainty maiden in his skinny arms and stalked forward into his abode with never a backward glance at the indecisive Po Ko.

The Emperor didn't know what to do. He hung back, carelessly knocking a nose off one of the statues with a thrown pebble. (He had really aimed for the jewelled eyes, but his long nails had spoilt the cast.) Then he decided to follow Chen yu into the palace . . . but what was he to say to this dark, crooked creature? How could he get the Jewel of Power from him? And were these statues really just things of hewn stone, or men transformed by magic and set here to warn off intruders?

The Magician was at the great portal of his dwelling. He strode within, and just as Po Ko had about made up his mind to stop him, the brassy door clanged shut in his face. Pei Wei was a prisoner within—how could he rescue her? Should he try, or go back to his capital and leave her to her unknown fate?

No; he would not. He retired to the shade of a flowering *kwaidphu* tree and dusted off a rock with his pine-scented kerchief and sat down. Stroking his forehead wearily, he pondered on his next step. "I will just sit here and wait for something to happen," he said, and quoted the ancient proverb, "the damned river does not flow to hell."

So he rested a long while and then with a metallic smash music blared from the Magician's palace. The massive doors swung wide and from the interior swarmed a horde of three-legged red imps with fiery eyes at the ends of long antennae. They all dragged upon a rope, tugging and groaning in rhythm to wailing melody, and at last hauled into sight a new statue, a horrid thing all sharp angles and flat planes. With pardonable difficulty, Po Ko recognized it as a crude caricature of Pei Wei.

As he watched curiously, the demons dragged the statue to an unoccupied pedestal at one end of the cave. Grunting and heaving, they hoisted it upon the pedestal, then danced around it, shrieking wildly. Was it really Pei Wei, metamorphosed into stone by magic, or a hastily cut likeness of her?

There was no way of telling; but now was his chance to slip into the palace while the imps were busy and the doors still open. Stealthily as a stalking puma he crept from the shade of the *kwaidphu* tree, and, with a wary backward look, he entered the palace. He sauntered down long halls like highways cut through forests of black marble pillars, until at last he found himself in Chen yu's throne room. But the Magician was seated on his dais, awaiting him. As Po Ko entered, Chen yu savagely struck a gong beside him, sending out rolling vibrations that tumbled through the corridors and outside, to reach the ears of the red prancing imps.

Shouting gleefully, they bounded within. It was a tense moment. Did they mean to devour Po Ko, or would he simply be turned into a grotesque statue? His knees knocked together in fear, his teeth chattered, his heart pounded and his hair stood on end, elevating his head-dress. He paled to a ghastly shade as he stood there trembling, wishing that he had never come.

Chen yu pointed a crooked forefinger at the stricken monarch. "Seize him!" he shrieked. Po Ko thought and acted simultaneously, but the trouble was that he thought one thing and did another. He started for a tall stair, at the same time running out of the door, which catapulted him straight into the Magician, overturning the throne and depositing the startled Chen yu among the bounding imps. "Attack him! Why don't you surge forward!" Chen yu screamed.

But the scrambling red imps, as they poured through the doorway, got tangled in each other's legs and this delay, getting various limbs unsorted, gave Po Ko time to make up his mind afresh—suiting his deeds to his thoughts, he sprinted up a tall stair. At once Chen yu's squalling cohorts were after him. Higher and higher he scrambled, with them close behind him. But there was no chance of escape. The stair led only to a balcony. Must he jump? It was death if he did—but a clean death. Better than letting Chen yu transform him into an ugly statue!

As he poised on the balustrade, something of his old dignity returned to him. He braced himself, cast a sneering look of contempt upon his pursuers, and uttered the philosophical proverb, "The gem which falls into the ocean gives forth beauty even though submerged!" His voice rang out, clear and virile, and then he leaped into space. The pavement rushed up to meet him. Even facing death, he was calm. He said (with difficulty, for the wind snatched the words from his mouth and blurred them), "The idiot smiles at the falling star, the wise man makes a wish!"

A lamp hung on a long cord from the balcony. Falling, Po Ko reached out, burned his hand on the cord, was stopped with a jerk by the lamp itself, and the impetus swung him to one side of the room. He dropped stunned to the floor, but the furious little imps were still piled up at the head of the stair far above, so he had time to scramble to his feet and dash out into the hall, looking for a hiding place.

As he darted from pillar to pillar, the devils searched for him, but he eluded them, and at last they went away, muttering under their breaths. And he was safe!

After a long time he ventured forth from his hiding-place, intent only on escaping this terrible palace. But as he passed out of the entrance, he spied the tiny black figure of Chen yu grovelling before the statue that looked like a cubist caricature of little Pei Wei. Chen yu weepingly decked the image with gems. "My love, my fair one!" he mourned, "be not disheartened. If you will renounce your lover, I will change you back to yourself!"

And—terribly—the statue spoke back in a harsh travesty of poor Pei Wei's dulcet voice. "I will remain true to my Po Ko."

The Emperor shuddered at this diabolic manifestation, and crept across the cavern floor to the *kwaidphu* tree. The imps had all vanished. Po Ko waited, and when the Magician had decked the effigy with jewels, and wiped away the last of his tears, and had gone slowly and sadly back into his palace, Po Ko emerged from hiding. There was nothing he could do for poor Pei Wei; so he decided to snatch away the jewels Chen yu had bedecked her with, and hurry back to his capital. Never would he meddle with sorcery again!

As he lifted away the first chain of flashing stones, he heard a vague crunching as if something heavy were being dragged over the ground. He turned, but saw no one, though it seemed that all the statues had moved a foot or so from their places. He unhooked a second necklace, and heard again the minatory sound. Now the idols were even closer. But how could that be? Magic—some trick of the crooked little sorcerer?

Even as he reached for the third string, he heard the sound. Yes, this time they had definitely moved. Their eyes shone with life! They were inching towards him, stone bases squealing over the glassy pave. If he hurried, Po Ko thought he could strip off the remaining gems. But then he heard a horrible travesty of Pei Wei's voice as before, saying "Oh, my Lord—wouldst forsake me?" Unnerved, Po Ko's clutching hand fell at his side. Closer and closer, inexorably, the statues bore down upon him.

With a shrill cry, all his dignity and pride forgotten, the Emperor snatched away the last strand of jewels. He heard a burst of strident laughter and turned. Chen yu stood on the palace steps, laughing horribly, shaking with mirth! But Po Ko was not deterred. Stuffing the last necklace within his robe, he leaped from the pedestal. As he did so a great stone drop, like a tear, struck his wrist. It had fallen from the *eyes* of the statue! The transformed damsel was weeping!

And now the statues were drawn in a tight ring, fencing him in. They were ranked so close, he could not get past them. He darted about, pushing aginst them, shrieking curses; and still they inched forward, stone bases digging scratches across the mirror pavement. Sides grating together, they leaned down over him, caging him in a stone cell. Unheeded, the necklaces fell from the bosom of his gown as he tugged and tore and hammered with futile fists against the glint-eyed shapes of unyielding rock.

And then the statues rocked on their bases, wobbled, tipped, and fell upon him, one by one. Dust swirled up and slowly settled. One long-nailed hand protruded bloodily from the heaped stone figures. It flapped weakly for an instant, and then lay still. Po Ko was dead.

As Chen yu sidled forward to gloat, out of the carven mouth of Pei Wei, who still occupied her pedestal, a sad, harsh voice uttered the ancient saying, "The miser throws away the flaming sun for a handful of cold stones."

Chen yu peered up. "Yes," he said indifferently, "words of wisdom falling from a woman's lips are like the beating of a gong in a temple of ten thousand silences."

Pei Wei said, "The man who steals a rose from a neighbor's garden, smells it once and casts it aside." For once, Chen yu could think of no reply.

Nevermore would his gilded palanquin bear him in splendor through the streets of his superb capital. Nevermore would he sprawl in his Monday throne, his Tuesday throne, his Wednesday throne—in fact, in any of his thrones. He was dead.

And only Pei Wei wept for him. She wept stony tears for him. Tear after tear, until a mound of smooth white pebbles hid her pedestal and her white stone feet.

L. Sprague de Camp

THE EMPEROR'S FAN

Sprague has been writing fantasy almost as long as Fritz Leiber has, and runs him a very close second for the title of best living fantasy writer. He has a light touch with fantasy that I have always found most pleasurable, and strikes a note of humor very welcome in a genre which is often grimly humorless, as with Howard's stories, for instance. This new story was written quite recently for a memorial anthology dedicated to John W. Campbell, Jr., who was the first editor to buy a de Camp story, and who bought most of the ones we remember most fondly. Although new, it has the rich imagination and light touch of vintage de Camp from the great years.

—LC

In the fifteenth year of his reign, Tsotuga the Fourth, Emperor of Kuromon, sat in the Forbidden Chamber of his Proscribed Palace, in his imperial city of Chingun. He played a game of Sachi with his crony, Reiro the beggar.

The pieces on one side were carved from single emeralds; those on the other, from single rubies. The board was of squares of onyx and gold. The many shelves and taborets in the room were crowded with small art objects. There were knicknacks of gold and silver, of ivory and ebony, of porcelain and pewter, of jasper and jade, of chrysoprase and chalcedony.

87

In a silken robe embroidered with lilies in silver thread and lotuses in golden thread, Tsotuga sat on a semi-throne —a chair of gilded mahogany, the arms of which were carven in the form of diamond-eyed dragons. The Emperor was plainly well fed, and within the hour he had been bathed and perfumed. Yet, although he had just won a game, Emperor Tsotuga was not happy.

"The trouble with you, chum," said Reiro the beggar, "is that, not having enough real dangers to worry about, you make up imaginary ones."

The Emperor took no offense. The purpose of the Forbidden Chamber was to afford him a place where he could treat and be treated by his crony as if they were ordinary human beings, without the court's stifling formality.

Nor was it an accident that Reiro was a beggar. As such, he would never try to intrigue against or murder his imperial friend in order to seize the throne.

Although a fairly competent ruler, Tsotuga was not a man of much personal charm. He was in fact rather dull save when, as sometimes happened, he lost his temper. Then he might visit dire dooms on those about him. After he had calmed down, Tsotuga would regret his injustice and might even pension the victim's dependents. He honestly tried to be just but lacked the self-control and objectivity to do so.

Reiro got along with the Emperor well enough. While the beggar cared nothing for art, save when he could filch and sell a piece of it, he was glad to listen to the Emperor's endless tales of his collection in return for the sumptuous repasts he enjoyed. Reiro had gained twenty pounds since he had become intimate with the Emperor.

"Oh, yes?" said Tsotuga. "That is easy for you to say. You are not nightly haunted by your father's ghost, threatening dreadful doom."

Reiro shrugged. "You knew the risk when you had the old man poisoned. It is all in the game, pal. For your pay, I would cheerfully submit to any number of nightmares. How does old Haryo look in these dreams?"

"The same old tyrant. I had to slay him—you know that—ere he ruined the Empire. But have a care with that flapping tongue."

"Nought I hear here goes beyond these walls. Anyway,

if you think Haryo's fate be not widely known, you do but befool yourself."

"I daresay it is suspected. But then, foul play is always suspected when an emperor dies. As said Dauhai to the timorous bird, every twig is a serpent.

"Still," continued the Emperor, "that solves not my problem. I wear mail beneath my robe. I sleep on a mattress floating in a pool of quicksilver. I have given up futtering my women, lest whilst I lie in their arms, some conspirator steal up and dagger me. The Empress, I can tell you, mislikes this abstinence. But still Haryo threatens and prophesies, and the warnings of a ghost are not to be flouted. I need some impregnable magical defense. That idiot Koxima does nought but fumigate and exorcize, which may drive out the demons but fails to blunt the steel of human foes. Have you any counsel, Ragbag?"

Reiro scratched. "There is a dark, beak-nosed, round-eyed old he-witch, hight Ajendra, lately come to Chingun from Mulvan. He gains a scanty living by selling love potions and finding lost bangles in trances. He claims to have a magical weapon of such power that none can stand against it."

"What is its nature?"

"He will not say."

"If he have so puissant a device, why is he not a king?"

"How could he make himself ruler? He is too old to lead an army in battle. Besides, he says that the holy order to which he belongs—all Mulvanian wizards call themselves holy men, be they never such rascals—forbids the use of this armament save in self-defense."

"Has anybody seen it?"

"Nay, chum; but rumor whispers that Ajendra has used it."

"Yes? And then what?"

"Know you a police spy named Nanka?"

The Emperor frowned. "Meseems—there was something about such a man who disappeared. It is supposed that the low company he kept at last learnt of his occupation and did him in."

The beggar chuckled. "Close, but not in the gold. This Nanka was a scoundrel of deepest dye, who supplemented his earnings as an informer by robbery and extortion. He skated into Ajendra's hut with the simple, wholesome intention of breaking the old man's neck and seizing Ajendra's rumored weapon."

"Hm. Well?"

"Well, Nanka never came out. A patrolman of the regular police found Ajendra sitting cross-legged in meditation and no sign of the erstwhile spy. Since Nanka was large and the hovel small, the corpse could not have been hidden. As it is said, the digger of pitfalls shall at last fall into one of his own."

"Hm," said Tsotuga. "I must look into this. Enough Sachi for the nonce. You must let me show you my latest acquisition!"

Reiro groaned inside and braced himself for an hour's lecture on the history and beauty of some antique bibelot. The thought of the palatial cookery, however, stiffened his resolve.

"Now, where did I put that little widget?" said Tsotuga, tapping his forehead with his folded fan.

"What is it, chum?" asked the beggar.

"A topaz statuette of the goddess Amarasupi, from the Jumbon Dynasty. Oh, curse my bowels with ulcers! I grow more absent-minded day by day."

"Good thing your head is permanently affixed to the rest of you! As the wise Ashuziri said, hope is a charlatan, sense a bungler, and memory a traitor."

"I distinctly remember," muttered the Emperor, "telling myself to put it in a special place where I should be sure to remember it. But now I cannot recall the special place."

"The Proscribed Palace must have ten thousand special places," said Reiro. "That is the advantage of being poor. One has so few possessions that one need never wonder where they are."

"Almost you tempt me to change places with you, but my duty forbids. Damn, damn, what did I with that silly thing? Oh, well, let us play another game instead. You take the red this time, I the green."

Two days later, Emperor Tsotuga sat on his throne of audience, wearing his towering crown of state. This plumed and winged headgear, bedight with peacock feathers and precious stones, weighed over ten pounds. It even had a secret compartment. Because of its weight,

Tsotuga avoided wearing it whenever he felt that he decently could.

The usher led in Ajendra. The Mulvanian magician was a tall, gaunt, bent old man, who supported himself on a stick. Save for the long white beard flowing down from his wrinkled, mahogany-hued face, he was brown all over, from dirty brown bulbous turban and dirty brown robe to dirty brown bare feet. His monotone contrasted with the golds and vermilions and greens and blues and purples of the Chamber of Audience.

In a cracked voice, speaking Kuromonian with an accent, Ajendra went through the formal greeting: "This wretched worm humbly abases himself before Thine Ineffable Majesty!" The wizard began, slowly and painfully, to get down on hands and knees.

The Emperor motioned him up, saying, "In respect for your years, old man, we will omit the prostration. Simply tell us about this invincible weapon of yours."

"Your Imperial Majesty is too kind to this unworthy wretch. See Your Majesty this?"

From his ragged sleeve, the Mulvanian produced a large painted fan. Like the others present, Ajendra kept his gaze averted from the Emperor's face, on the pretense that one who looked the ruler full in the face would be blinded by his awful glory.

"This," continued Ajendra, "was made for the king of the Gwoling Islands by the noted wizard Tsunjing. By a series of chances too long to bore Your Imperial Majesty with, it came into the unworthy hands of this inferior person."

At least, thought Tsotuga, the fellow had learnt the polite forms of Kuromonian address. Many Mulvanians were informal to the point of rudeness. Aloud he said, "It looks like any other fan. What is its power?"

"Simple, O superior one. Any living thing that you fan with it disappears."

"Oho!" exclaimed the Emperor. "So that is what befell the missing Nanka!"

Ajendra looked innocent. "This loathsome reptile does not understand Your Divine Majesty."

"Never mind. Whither go the victims!"

"One theory of my school is that they are translated to a higher dimension, coexistent with this one. Another holds that they are dispersed into constituent atoms, which, however, retain such mutual affinities that they can be reassembled when the signal for recall is—"

"Mean you that you can reverse the effect and fetch back the vanished beings?"

"Aye, superhuman sire. One folds the fan and taps one's wrists and forehead according to a simple code, and presto! there is the evanished one. Would Your Majesty see a demonstration? There is no danger to the demonstratee, since this humble person can bring him back instanter."

"Very well, good wizard. Just be careful not to wave that thing at us. On whom propose you to try it?"

Ajendra looked about the Chamber of Audience. There was a stir amongst ushers, guardsmen and officials. Light winked on gilded armor and glowed on silken robes as each tried to make himself inconspicuous behind a pillar or another courtier.

"Who will volunteer?" asked the Emperor. "You, Dzakusan?"

The Prime Minister prostrated himself. "Great Emperor, live forever! This lump of iniquity has not been well lately. Moreover, he has nine children to support. He humbly begs Your Supremacy to excuse him."

Similar questions to other functionaries produced similar responses. At length Ajendra said, "If this lowly one may make a suggestion to Your Magnificence, it might be better to try it first on a beast—say, a dog or a cat."

"Aha!" said Tsotuga. "Just the thing. We know the animal, too. Surakai, fetch that cursed dog belonging to the Empress—you know, that yapping little monstrosity."

The messenger departed on his roller skates. Soon he was back, leading on a leash a small woolly white dog, which barked incessantly.

"Go ahead," said the Emperor.

"This negligible person hears and obeys," said Ajendra, opening the fan.

The dog's yelp was cut off as the draft from the fan struck it. Surakai trailed an empty leash. The courtiers started and murmured.

"By the Heavenly Bureaucrats!" exclaimed the Emperor. "That is impressive. Now bring the creature back.

Fear not if you fail. The thing has bitten us twice, so the Empire will not fall if it remain in that other dimension."

Ajendra produced from his other sleeve a small codex, whose pages he thumbed. Then he held a reading glass to his eye. "Here it is," he said. " 'Dog. Two left, three right, one to head.' "

Having folded the fan, Ajendra, holding it in his right hand, rapped his left wrist twice. Transferring the fan to his left hand, he then tapped his right wrist thrice and his forehead once. Instantly the dog reappeared. Yapping, it fled under the throne.

"Very good," said the Emperor. "Leave the creature where it is. What is that, a code book?"

"Aye, supreme sire. It lists all the categories of organic beings subject to the fan's power."

"Well, let us try it on a human being—an expendable one. Mishuho, have we a condemned criminal handy?"

"Live forever, incomparable one!" said the Minister of Justice. "We have a murderer due to lose his head to-morrow. Shall this miserable creature fetch him?"

The murderer was fetched. Ajendra fanned him out of existence and tapped him back again.

"Whew!" said the murderer. "This contemptible one must have suffered a dizzy spell."

"Where were you whilst you were vanished?" said the Emperor.

"I knew not that I was vanished, great Emperor!" said the murderer. "I felt dizzy and seemed to lose my wits for an instant—and then here I was, back in the Proscribed Palace."

"Well, you disappeared, all right. In consideration of his services to the state, Mishuho, commute his sentence to twenty-five lashes and turn him loose. Now, Doctor Ajendra!"

"Aye, ruler of the world?"

"What are the limitations of your fan? Does it run out of charge and have to be resorceled?"

"Nay, exalted one. At least, its power has not weakened in the centuries since Tsunjing made it."

"Does it work on a large animal, say a horse or an elephant?"

"It does better than that. When the grandson of the Gwoling king for whom it was made, Prince Wangerr, met a dragon on Banshou Island, he swept the monster out of existence with three mighty strokes of the fan."

"Hm. Quite powerful enough, it seems. Now, good Ajendra, suppose you bring back that police spy, Nanka, on whom you employed your arts a few days ago!"

The Mulvanian shot a glance at the Emperor's face. Some courtiers murmured at this breach of decorum, but Tsotuga seemed not to notice. The wizard evidently satisfied himself that the ruler knew whereof he spoke. Ajendra thumbed through his book until he came to "Spy." Then he tapped his left wrist four times and his forehead twice.

A big, burly man in beggar's rags materialized. Nanka was still wearing the roller skates on which he had entered Ajendra's hut. Unprepared as he was for this appearance, his feet flew out from under him. He fell heavily on his back, cracking his head on the red-white-and-black tessellated marble floor. The Emperor laughed heartily, and the courtiers allowed themselves discreet smiles.

As the informer, red with rage and astonishment, climbed to his feet, Tsotuga said, "Mishuho, give him ten lashes for trying to rob a subject. Tell him that next time it will be his head—if not the boiling oil. Take him away. Well now, worthy wizard, what would you have for your device and its code book?"

"Ten thousand golden dragons," said Ajendra, "and an escort to my own country."

"Hm. Is that not a lot for a holy ascetic?"

"It is not for myself that this humble being asks," said the Mulvanian. "I would build and endow a temple to my favorite gods in my native village. There I shall pass my remaining days in meditation on the Thatness of the All."

"A meritorious project," said Tsotuga. "Let it be done. Chingitu, see that Doctor Ajendra has a trustworthy escort to Mulvan. Have them get a letter from the King of Kings, testifying that they delivered Ajendra safely and did not murder him for his gold along the way."

"This despicable one hears and obeys," said the Minister of War.

For the next month, things went smoothly at court. The Emperor kept his temper. No one, knowing of the

magical fan that the testy monarch carried, cared to
provoke him. Even Empress Nasako, although furious at
her husband's callous use of her dog, kept her sharp
tongue sheathed. Tsotuga remembered where he had hidden the statuette of Amarasupi and so for a time was
almost happy.

But, as said the philosopher Dauhai back in the Jumbon
Dynasty, everything passes away. The day came when,
in the Emperor's study, Minister of Finance Yaebu tried
to explain the workings of that marvelous new invention, paper money. The Emperor demanded to know
why he could not simply abolish all taxes, thus pleasing
the people, and pay the government's bills with newly
printed currency notes. Tsotuga was irascible as a re-
sult of having mislaid another of his prized antique gim-
cracks.

"But, Your Divine Majesty!" wailed Yaebu. "That was
tried in Gwoling, half a century ago! The value of the
notes dropped to nought. None would offer aught for
sale, since none wished to accept worthless paper. They
had to go back to barter."

"We should think a few heads on poles would have
fixed that," growled Tsotuga.

"The then king of Gwoling tried that, too," said Yaebu.
"It accomplished nought; the markets remained empty of
goods. City folk starved . . ."

The argument continued while the Emperor, who had
little head for economics, became more and more rest-
less, bored, and impatient. Ignoring these signs, Yaebu
persisted in his arguments.

At last the Emperor exploded, "Curse your arse with
boils, Yaebu! We will show you how to keep saying 'nay'
and 'however' and 'impossible' to your *sovran!* Begone,
sirrah!"

Tsotuga whipped out his fan, snapped it open, and
fanned a blast of air at Yaebu. The minister vanished.

Hm, mused Tsotuga, *it really does work. Now I must
fetch Yaebu back, for I did not really mean to destroy
the faithful fellow. It is just that he irritates me so with his
everlasting "if's" and "but's" and "can't's." Let me see,
where did I put that code book? I remember hiding it in
a special place where I could be sure of finding it again.
But where?*

The Emperor looked first in the deep, baggy sleeves' of his embroidered silken robe, which in Kuromon served the office of pockets. It was not there.

Then the Emperor rose from his business throne and went to the imperial wardrobe, where a hundred-odd robes hung from pegs. There were silken robes for official use, thin for summer and quilted for winter. There were woolen robes for outdoor winter use and cotton robes for outdoor summer use. They were dyed scarlet and emerald, saffron and azure, cream and violet, and all the other colors in the dyers' armory.

Tsotuga went down the line, feeling in the sleeves of each robe. A tireman hurried in, saying, "O Divine Autocrat, permit this filthy beggar to relieve you of this menial chore!"

Tsotuga: "Nay, good Shakatabi; we entrust this task to none but ourselves."

Laboriously, Tsotuga continued down the line until he had examined all the robes. Then he began the rounds of the Proscribed Palace, pulling out the drawers of desks and dressers, poking into cubbyholes, and shouting for the keys to chests and strongboxes.

After several hours, exhaustion forced the Emperor to desist. Falling into the semi-throne of the Forbidden Chamber, he struck the gong. When the room was jampacked with servants, he said, "We, Tsotuga the Fourth, offer a reward of a hundred golden dragons to him who finds the missing code book that goes with our miraculous fan!"

That day, the Proscribed Palace saw a great scurrying and searching. Scores of felt-slippered servants shuffled about, opening, poking, prying and peering. When night fell, the book had not been found.

Beshrew me! said Tsotuga to himself. *Poor Yaebu is lost unless we find the accursed book. I must be more careful with that fan.*

Again, as spring advanced, things went smoothly for awhile. But the day came when Tsotuga was roller-skating about the paths of the palace gardens with Minister of War Chingitu. Questioned sharply about the recent defeat of the Kuromonian army by the nomads of the steppes, Chingitu offered excuses that Tsotuga knew to be mendacious. Away went Tsotuga's temper. "The real reason," roared the Emperor, "is that your cousin, the Quartermaster-General, has been grafting and filling posts with his worthless relatives, so that our soldiers were ill-armed! And you know it! Take that!"

A wave of the fan, and no more Chingitu. In like manner, shortly thereafter, perished Prime Minister Dzakusan.

The want of properly appointed ministers soon made itself felt. Tsotuga could not personally supervise all the hundreds of bureaucrats in the now-headless departments. These civil servants devoted themselves more and more to feuding, loafing, nepotism and peculation. Conditions were bad in Kuromon anyway, because of the inflation brought about by Tsotuga's paper-money scheme. The government was fast becoming a shambles.

"You must pull yourself together, lord," said Empress Nasako, "ere the pirates of the Gwoling Archipelago and the brigands from the steppes divide Kuromon between them, as a man divides an orange."

"But what in the name of the fifty-seven major deities shall I do?" cried Tsotuga. "Curse it, if I had that code book, I could bring back Yaebu, who would straighten out this financial mess."

"Oh, forget the book. If I were you, I should burn that magical fan ere it got me into more trouble."

"You are out of your mind, woman! Never!"

Nasako sighed. "As the sage Zuiku said, who would use a tiger for a watchdog to guard his wealth will soon need neither wealth nor watchdog. At least appoint a new prime minister, to bring order out of this chaos."

"I have gone over the list of possible candidates, but every one has a black mark against him. One was connected with that faction that conspired my assassination nine years ago. Another was accused of grafting, although it was never proved. Still another is ailing—"

"Is Zamben of Jompei on your list?"

"I have never heard of him. Who is he?"

"The supervisor of roads and bridges in Jade Mountain Province. They say he has made an excellent record there."

"How know you about him?" snapped the Emperor suspiciously.

"He is a cousin of my first lady-in-waiting. She has long urged his virtues upon me. I brushed her suit aside, knowing my lord's dislike of letting my ladies exploit their position by abetting their kinsmen's interests. In your present predicament, though, you could do worse than look the fellow over."

"Very well, I will."

Thus it happened that Zamben of Jompei became prime minister. The former supervisor of roads and bridges was younger by a decade than the Emperor. He was a handsome, cheerful, charming, rollicking person who made himself popular with the court, save for those determined to hate the favorite of the moment. Tsotuga thought Zamben was rather too light-hearted and lacking in respect for the labyrinthine etiquette. But Zamben proved an able administrator who soon had the vast governmental machine running smoothly.

But it is said that the thatcher's roof is the leakiest in the village. What the Emperor did not know was that Zamben and Empress Nasako were secret lovers. They had been before Zamben's elevation. Circumstances made it hard to consummate their passion, save rarely in one of Nasako's summer pavilions in the hills.

In the Proscribed Palace, it was even harder. The palace swarmed with menials who would be glad to carry tales. The amorous pair had to resort to stratagems. Nasako announced that she had to be left entirely alone in a summer house to compose a poem. The versatile Zamben wrote the poem for her as evidence before he hid himself in the summer house in advance of her arrival.

"That was worth waiting for," said the Empress, donning her garments. "That fat old fool Tsotuga has not touched me in a year, and a full-blooded woman like me needs frequent stoking. He has not even futtered his pretty young concubines, albeit he is not yet fifty."

"Why? Is he prematurely senile?"

"Nay; it is his fear of assassination. For awhile, he tried doing it in the seated position, so that he could keep looking about for possible assailants. But since he insisted on wearing his armor, it proved too awkward to please anyone. So he gave it up altogether."

"Well, the thought of a stab in the back is depressing to more than just a man's spirit. If—which the gods forfend—an accident should befall His Divine Majesty—"

"How?" said Nasako. "No assassin dares approach him whilst he has that fan."

"Where does he put it at night?"

"Under his pillow, and he sleeps clutching it. It would take a winged demon to get at him anyway, floating in that pool of quicksilver."

"A hard-driven crossbow bolt, shot from beyond the fan's range—"

"Nay, he is too well guarded to let an arbalester get within range, and he even sleeps in his mail."

"Well, we shall see," said Zamben. "Meanwhile, Nako, how would my love like another?"

"What a man you are!" cried Nasako, beginning to cast off her just donned garments.

During the next two months, the court noted that Zamben, not content with being the second most powerful man in the Empire, had also ingratiated himself with the Emperor. He did so well as to oust Reiro the beggar from his position as Emperor's crony. Zamben even became an expert on the history of art, the better to admire Tsotuga's prized gewgaws.

The favorite-haters at court muttered that for an emperor to make a personal friend of a minister was a violation of sound method. Not only was the mystical balance among the Five Elements upset, but also Zamben might entertain usurpatory notions, which his friendship might enable him to put into effect. But none dared to broach the subject to the explosive-tempered Tsotuga. They shrugged, saying, "After all, it is the Empress's duty to warn him. If she cannot, what chance have we?"

Zamben went his smiling way, smoothly running the government by day and fraternizing with the Emperor by night.

At last came his opportunity. The Emperor was toying with his fan over a game of Sachi. Zamben dropped a piece—an elephant—on the floor so that it rolled under the table.

"Let me get it," said Tsotuga. "It is on my side."

As he bent to fumble for the piece, he dropped his fan. He straightened up holding the piece, to find Zamben holding the fan out to him. Tsotuga snatched it back. "Excuse my discourtesy," said the Emperor, "but I am fain not to let that thing out of my hands. It was stupid of me not to have put it away ere reaching for your elephant. It is still your move."

Days later, in the summer house, Empress Nasako asked, "Did you get it?"

"Aye," replied Zamben. "It was no trick to hand him the duplicate."

"Then what are you waiting for? Fan the old fool away!"

"Tut, tut, my sweet. I must assure the loyalty of my partisans. It is said that he who would swallow a pumpkin with one bite shall reap the reward of his gluttony. Besides, I have scruples."

"Oh, pish-tush! Are you just a pillow-warrior, strong in the yard but weak in the sword arm?"

"Nay, but I am a careful man who avoids offending the gods or biting off more than he can chew. Hence I would fan away only one who tried to do me ill. Knowing your imperial spouse, madam, I am sure he will soon force me to defend myself."

The evening came when Zamben, whose skill at Sachi had never seemed remarkable, suddenly beat the Emperor five games in a row.

"Curse you!" bawled Tsotuga as he lost his fifth king. "Have you been taking lessons? Or were you more skilled all along than you seemed?"

Zamben grinned and spread his hands. "The Divine Bureaucrats must have guided my moves."

"You—you—" Tsotuga choked with rage. "We will show you how to mock your emperor! Begone from the world!"

The Emperor whipped out his fan and fanned, but Zamben failed to disappear. Tsotuga fanned some more. "Curse it, has this thing lost its charge?" said Tsotuga. "Unless it be not the real—"

His sentence was cut off as Zamben, opening the true magical fan, swept the Emperor out of existence. Later,

Zamben explained to the Empress, "I knew that, when he found that his fan did not work, he would suspect a substitution. So there was nought to do but use the real one."

"What shall we tell the court and the people?"

"I have thought all that out. We will give out that, plagued by the summer's heat, in an absent-minded moment he fanned himself."

"Would it work that way?"

"I know not; who were so rash as to try it? In any case, after a decent interval of mourning, I shall expect you to carry out your end of the bargain."

"Right willingly, my love."

Thus it came to pass that the widowed Empress wedded Zamben of Jompei, after the latter had, at her demand, put away his two previous wives. The minister acquired the courtesy title of "Emperor" but not the full powers of that office. Technically he was the consort of the Dowager Empress and guardian of and regent for the heir.

As to what would happen when the fourteen-year-old Prince Wakumba reached his majority, Zamben did not worry. He was sure that, whatever betide, he could charm the young Emperor into continuing his power and perquisites.

He thought of having the Prince murdered but quickly put that plan aside. For one thing, he feared that Nasako would have him killed in turn, for her supporters far outnumbered his. He had a hard enough task, just keeping on good terms with her. She was disillusioned to find that in her new husband she had obtained, not an ever-panting satyr, but merely an ambitious politician so immersed in political maneuvers, administrative details and religious rituals that he had little time and strength left over for stoking her fires. When she complained, he spoke of his "essential new project."

"What is that?" she demanded.

"I will not," he said, "waste more time in searching for that code book. Instead, I shall reconstruct the code by trial and error."

"How?"

"I shall try combinations of raps and note what I get

each time. In the centuries that the fan has existed, hundreds of beings must have been fanned away."

The next day Zamben, flanked by six heavily armed palace guards, sat in the Chamber of Audience, which had been cleared of all others save two secretaries. Zamben tapped his left wrist once. A beggar appeared on the floor before him.

The beggar screamed with terror and fainted. When the man had been revived, it was found that he had been fanned out of existence more than a century before, in a fishing village on the shore of the ocean. He was astounded suddenly to find himself in a palace.

Zamben commanded, "Write: one tap on left wrist, beggar. Give him one golden dragon and show him out."

Two taps on the left wrist produced a swineherd, and so it was recorded. During the day, persons of all sorts were rapped into existence. Once a leopard appeared, snarling. Two guardsmen rushed upon it, but it sprang out the open window and vanished.

Some combinations of raps failed to bring results. Either they were not connected with victims of any definite kind, or no beings of that kind had ever been fanned away and not recalled.

"All right so far," said Zamben to the Empress that night.

"What if your experiments bring back Tsotuga?"

"By the fifty-seven major deities, I had not thought of that! An emperor, I suppose, needs a combination of many taps to bring him back. The instant I see him, I will fan him back to limbo."

"Have a care! I am sure that fan will sooner or later bring evil upon him who uses it."

"Fear not; I shall be cautious."

The next day, the experiments continued and the secretaries' lists of formulae lengthened. Three taps each on left wrist, right wrist, and forehead produced the missing Finance Minister Yaebu, much shaken.

Following Yaebu came an ass and a fuller. When the ass had been captured and led out, and the fuller had been soothed and sent away with his fee, Zamben tapped his left and right wrists each three times and his forehead four times.

There was a rush of displaced air. Filling most of the Chamber of Audience was a dragon. Zamben, his jaw sagging, started to rise. The dragon roared and roared, and the guards fled clattering.

Through Zamben's mind flashed a tale he had heard about the fan. Centuries before, it had saved the Gwoling prince Wangerr from a dragon on Banshou Island. This must be the same . . .

Zamben began to open the fan, but astonishment and terror had paralyzed him a few seconds too long. The great, scaly head swooped; the jaws slammed shut.

The only person left in the chamber was one of the secretaries, cowering behind the throne. This man heard a single scream. Then the dragon hunched itself out the window, with a crashing of broken window frame and—since the aperture was still too small for it—of a goodly part of the wall. The scribe peeked around the throne to see the scaly tail vanishing through the jagged gap that yawned where the window had been, and a cloud of brick and plaster dust filling the Chamber of Audience.

Yaebu and Nasako became co-regents. Lacking a man, the lusty Dowager Empress took up with a handsome groom from the imperial stables, half her age but well equipped to pleasure her, having no thoughts to distract him from his sexual duties. Yaebu, a conservative family man with no lust for exalted adultery, became prime minister. He ran the Empire in a somewhat hesitant, bumbling way but not unsuccessfully.

Since there was no emperor, even a nominal one, young Prince Wakumba had to be enthroned forthwith. After the day-long ceremony, the lad slowly pulled off the plumed and winged crown of state. He complained, "This thing seems even heavier than usual." He poked about inside it.

Yaebu hovered anxiously, murmuring, "Have a care, my liege! Watch out that you harm not that holy headgear!"

Something went *spung*, and a metal flap snapped up inside the crown.

"Here is that secret compartment," said Wakumba, "with a—what is this?—a book in it. By the fifty-seven divinities, this must be that code book that Dad was hunting!"

"Let me see!" cried Yaebu and Nasako together.

"That is it, all right. But since the dragon ate the fan along with my stepfather, the book is of no use. Let it be put in the archives with other curios."

Nasako said, "We must ask Kozima to make another magical fan, so that the book shall again be useful."

It is not, however, recorded that the court wizard of Kuromon ever succeeded in this endeavor. For aught I know, the code book still reposes peacefully in the Kuromonian archives in Chingun, and those who, like Tsotuga and Dzakusan, were fanned away and never brought back, still await their deliverance.

Pat McIntosh

FALCON'S MATE

*The first "gal Conan" in the history of Sword &
Sorcery was C. L. Moore's immortal Jirel of Joiry.
But here Jirel meets her match, in this first story
about Thula, mercenary swordswoman of an order
of warrior maids called the Order of the Moon. A
first story by a new British writer bound to go places
in the years to come!*

"Poor Thula," said Aneka from her big leather-cur-
tained horse-litter. "Is your headache any better?"

That, oddly enough, decided me. My headache was
definitely her fault. I made some answer, and reined in my
horse to let the big litter lurch through the archway into
the inn-yard, nodding to her cousin where he sat his raw-
boned bay horse bawling instructions at the pack-drivers.
He ignored me.

"Do you go up," I said to Aneka. "I'll stable my
horse."

"Gelen says they serve in half an hour," she said, jumping down in a swirl of embroidered petticoats. I nodded
and led my big grey Dester into the stable. Unsaddling
and brushing him down with soothing, accustomed movements, I considered the matter.

If she had drugged my wine, it was with a purpose. I
could think of two, but dismissed one. I had lived among
girls of my own age or younger since I was seven: if she
had done it out of sheer mischief, Aneka of all girls would

105

have shown it, by secret smiles and giggles. And yet the other was incredible. Three nights running, the door had been locked, the key under my pillow, the open window at least four fathoms above ground with nothing to tie a rope to: Master Gelen took these precautions, not I think out of suspicion but simply to safeguard valuable merchandise. And when I woke in the morning, Aneka had been sound asleep, sprawled on her bed with the covers kicked back and her nightshift under her arms, an abandoned pose which did not suggest a fond farewell at the door, and replacing the key under my pillow.

And yet, three mornings running, I had woken with a mouth like the floor of a birdcage, and a cleaver in my skull.

"Perhaps he can fly," I said to Dester. He snorted, and nudged me impatiently. I returned to my task, and determined on two things before I had finished. In the first place, Aneka would have my wine tonight, and I hers: and in the second, I would watch all night with my sword drawn.

Aneka was delighted when I arrived with my sword balanced on top of my saddlebags.

"What are you going to do?" she demanded. "Will you practise? Has it a name?"

"Her name is *Fenala*," I said rather shortly. I had forgotten until I drew the blade, that it was not my own familiar one of blue Southron steel; that lay on Fenala's breast in the tomb beside the village temple, away beyond Rhawn Dys. "She needs to be oiled," I said. This was partly true. "There isn't room to practise here."

"Show me!" said Aneka, kneeling beside me in three petticoats and no shoes. "There's writing! What does it say?"

I turned the blade on my knee, and spelled out the ancient letters with difficulty.

"*Niachan len dova*," I read at length. "A friend has two edges."

"A friend has two edges," she repeated, "what does it mean?"

"I don't know," I said. "It's a very old sword. You'd better dress, it's nearly dinner time."

She leapt up with a squeal that started my headache again, and seized another petticoat. I set down the sword, and began to remove my travel-stained clothes. They had brought warm water to wash with; Aneka had used most of it, as usual.

"Can you read?" she demanded through the final petticoat.

"Well, of course I can," I said. "And write. They teach us, in the Order."

"Oh, of course, the Order," she said. "Mama says reading's unfeminine."

"You surprise me," I said, rather drily. She lifted her brown-and-gold dress and pulled it over her head; it matched her hair, which was braided down her back after the custom of Rhawn Dys. I thought for the manyth time what a pity it was she should go to Dervir, where the ladies went powdered and corseted, in dresses ever richer than their neighbors'.

"I expect my husband wouldn't like it if I could read," she said complacently, smoothing the dress down. I reached for my clean shirt. "Don't you want to be married, Thula? Although I expect it's a bit late now, I mean, you're twenty-one." She made it sound as if I would soon be fifty.

"There was a girl left at thirty to get married," I said, a little defensively. She made round eyes.

"My sister was younger than me when she married," she said. "Mama says a man should be twice your age when you marry. Did that girl marry a man of sixty?"

"I doubt it," I said, rather sharply, doing up my tunic.

"My husband's thirty-two," she said, brushing out her hair. "Gelen says he's very handsome, but I think he should be a bit younger, say about twenty-seven."

Something in her tone made me say, "Do you want to marry him?"

In the mirror her lips moved, but the sound was drowned by a banging at the door.

"Ladies!" shouted the cousin. "Are you ready?"

"Nearly!" squeaked 'Aneka, braiding her hair with rapid expert fingers. Snatching a ribbon she wound it quickly round the ends and knotted it, and I straightened my tunic, stuck my dagger in my belt where it belonged and opened the door.

"We are ready, goodsir," I said; he bowed, averting his eyes from my trousered legs, and offered his arm to

Aneka. Curtsying, she accepted its support. I followed them down the stairs, wondering if I had seen right. In the mirror, Aneka's answer to my question had looked very like *No*.

After dinner we played the game of Siege. It is a board game, where one player defends a corner of the board against the other, the number of the pieces depending on the skill of the players. It is more common in the East-lands than here in the West; they often use it as a ritual means of making temple-offerings. I beat Aneka, and after a long game her cousin; as he cleared the pieces he said quietly, "You and Aneka should have another game, mistress. I am sure she will win this one."

"Are you?" I said.

"So am I!" said Aneka, overhearing. Come on, Thula! It's barely dark. Moonrise isn't for hours yet. You won our last match, so you lose a man, and it's my turn to defend."

I set up the pieces reluctantly. I was tired, and the cousin seemed to be expecting me to give her the game. Against a player like Aneka this is not easy: she played badly, but she was astute enough to see when I made foolish moves deliberately. And, since the game is sacred to the Moon, it was scarcely proper to reduce it to an amusement for a merchant's spoiled daughter in this way. I won. Aneka was annoyed, and showed it.

"We're playing another one," she said. "And I'm going to win."

"It's bedtime," I said, "and I've played three games in a row. Leave it till tomorrow night, Aneka."

"No," she said, "because tomorrow—" She paused, and changed what she was going to say. "Tomorrow you'll be fresh again and now you're tired. I'm sure I'll win!"

I was indeed tired, and my headache had returned. It was a long game, but at last Aneka said,

"In three moves, Thula, I've got you!"

"You have?" I said, startled. She crowed with delight.

"Yes, I have! See, my captain moves there, and this soldier here, and this one here, and you can't block any of them, and then I'm in the castle."

Master Gelen crossed the room to see the board, and said, "That's right, Aneka. That's the Falcon's Mate. I taught it you, remember."

"So it is," she marvelled. "And you said only a clever player could use it properly!"

"Now you have your revenge," I said, "and I agree it was cleverly done, are we going to bed?"

There was a jug of wine and two glasses set on the kist between the beds. To make things easy, I went to the window and leaned out. The courtyard was five fathoms down, and sheer; only a fly could climb the wall. I turned, and Aneka was sitting on her bed, sipping wine. I went and sat down too, and then said.

"Your hair's a funny colour. I wonder if it's going grey."

"Grey?" she said. "No! It can't be!" She set down her wine, some of it slopping over, and ran to the nearest box, delving in frantic haste for a mirror. I put my glass in the ring hers had made, and took hers in my hand; she got out the mirror and began peering anxiously, using the mirror over the wash-stand to see the back of her head.

"Perhaps it's just the light," I said, reassuringly. "Or the dust. Your colour hair does look funny in candle-light sometimes."

"Well it looks all right now," she said. "You frightened me."

In ten minutes she was asleep, half undressed. I finished the task, with difficulty, and covered her up; then I went to the window again, and on a sudden impulse took my naked sword and wedged it across the aperture, the sharper edge outward. Then I took my dagger in my hand, blew out the candle, and sat crosslegged on my bed to wait for dawn. Or was I waiting for moonrise?

And what would come then anyway? I began to feel that perhaps I was acting foolishly. I comforted myself with the thought that if I was, no one would know, except perhaps Aneka, and went over the facts again. I had thought this was a good way to cross the Old Mountains safely and be paid for doing it: There are lone war-maids but I am not one of them and Fenala was too recently dead for my own company to be a good thing. We had never been lovers, as I believe some pairs are, but we had been inseparable since I was eight and she nine and the gap made by her death—

I dragged myself sharply from that train of thought. It

led, as I well knew, to endless fits of weeping, and this was no time for tears. I had wept enough to fill an ocean, those weeks at the Temple in Rhawn Dys while I waited for another pair to come in, or a lone girl like me who wanted company. Then Mother Superior had sent for me, and described this task: Enys ma Doarrh ma Enys required a chaperone-bodyguard for his daughter, ten gold pieces to me and ten to the Order if she reached her husband as she left her father's house. It had seemed simple enough when I accepted.

Through the window I could see stars. They moved slowly past my sword, and at length the moon rose and threw silver on the wall. I began to feel numb, and tried to move, and could not. Panic rose in my throat as I tried unavailing to move so much as an eyelid. For what seemed an eternal year I struggled, and then a voice spoke.

"Aneka," it said. "Are you watching, little love? She will not wake, I have a keeping-spell on her. Are you watching, Aneka?"

I would have spoken, but I could not. Aneka never moved. Wings swished, and a great dark shape floated across the patch of sky.

"Aneka," said the voice. "It's Fenist—the moon has risen. Wake and let me in, love, for she has barred the window. Are you waking, Aneka?"

Still I could not answer him; and Aneka never moved. Again the wings swished, and the dark shape was at the window. Talons scrabbled on the sill, square-tipped wings beat and fluttered, a small sound of pain came on the night air.

"Aneka!" he said, desperately now. "Her sword at the window cuts me to the bone! Aneka, this night of all nights, wake and let me in, for I bleed here in the darkness— *Aneka!*"

I truly think, if I could have stirred, I would have risen and let him in; but he had bespelled me, and Aneka never moved. There was a silence, in which I heard breathing surely harsher than a bird's, and something splashed on the sill. Then he said,

"Aneka, I called you three times, and you did not answer, and tonight I was to bear you away. If you will not come to me by your will, you shall come by mine."

The dark wings, edged with moonlight, moved in the patch of sky, swished into the distance and were gone. And I was left waiting, numb with grief as with his spell. The pleading in his voice had touched my heart; just so had I pleaded with Fenala, to wake and turn to me and answer me, and she never moved.

I pulled myself together. That was no solitary warmaid, but a shape-shifter who had seduced an innocent maid destined for another man, instructed her to make me sleep, maybe even gave her the stuff to put in my wine. And what had they been doing while I slept——? I made an involuntary movement to reject that thought, and discovered I could move again. Jumping up I ran to the window and got my sword in. There was blood on the blade, still warm, and great drops of it gleaming faintly in the moonlight lying on the sill.

I cleaned my sword and sheathed it, and undressed slowly and lay down. But for a long time I could not sleep. Two voices rang in my head. One was Fenist's, the shape-shifter's:

"If you do not come to me by your will, you shall come by mine."

The other was my own, reading the words on my sword. A friend has two edges, it said. How should a person have two edges? Should a sword be my only friend? Certainly, if one got involved with people one got involved in problems . . .

The thunder that woke me diminished, and became Master Gelen banging on the door. I answered something, and he went away, and I got out of bed. Aneka lay heavily asleep, as if she had not stirred all night. My eye lit on my sword, propped beside the bed, and the events of the night rushed into my mind. Mother of mares, I prayed, give me strength to dissemble. I cannot lie, and you know it . . . I bent to shake Aneka awake.

There was no chance to dissemble. She roused slowly, but I saw the point at which she realised she had missed him. She leapt out of bed, despite the way it must have pained her head, and ran to the window and flung it wide. She stared out, east and then west at the Mountains looming closer, and then her gaze fell on the dried blood on the sill. She froze for a moment: then she began to scream.

We were late leaving. Aneka was still in hysterics, although by now these were mercifully reduced to a dry sobbing and occasional moans of "Traitor!" I had not attempted to argue, but concentrated on getting her into the litter. The cousin's enquiries I had stopped with a significant glance at the moon, just vanishing behind the Mountains. It was plausible enough: he was scarcely likely to know when her last moon-day had been. Since half the column of pack-horses had already moved off, her boxes were heaved into the litter beside her, and she lay sobbing among them with the curtains closed. I felt for her, but I could see no other course than to take her to her husband and hope she could be taught enough to fool him on his wedding night. We rode out of the inn-yard, and up the dusty road that led to the North Pass: the two big horses bearing the litter made good speed and I riding beside them on my grey Dester kept them up.

The pack-train reached the approaches to the pass before noon. The road rose up in coils about the grey dusty heights, bare of grass and heather. We rode more slowly now, but by mid-afternoon we had crossed the first, false summit and as the road wound we caught occasional glimpses of the High House, where we would spend the night. The road itself was narrow: the column had long since shuffled into single file and I was riding ahead of the litter, the last dozen or so pack-horses behind it, when Aneka put her head out and informed me, with the icy adolescent dignity, that she wished to go behind a bush.

"There aren't any here," I said. "It'll have to be a rock." I reined back and halted the litter, and the pack-horses picked their way past, the drivers grumbling as the horses slithered in the stony ground. Aneka emerged from the litter and found a suitable rock: when she emerged from behind it, sometime later, the tail of the column was well out of sight and the head was already appearing round the curve beyond. As she climbed back into the litter a shadow crossed the sun, and I could have sworn I heard the swish of wings: but when I looked up the sky was clear and empty. I whipped up the two big horses, and they achieved a lumbering trot: we thudded up to the corner and round it, into a cutting where the road widened to its original size. My Dester shied, and tossed his head, unwilling to go on.

"What is it, stupid?" I asked him, urging him on with knees and heels, using the whip in both hands alternately, on him and on the litter-horses. He squealed and half reared, swinging round into the lead horse, and there was a rumbling and crashing of thunder above us, and suddenly the defile before us was full of rocks, great boulders, pebbles, earth, and a choking dust that rose above everything. The lead horse, already alarmed by Dester, screamed in panic and tried to back and run away both at once. The other horse backed too, and somehow, I don't know how, the next thing was the two litter-horses bolting back down the road away from me, the litter jerking and swaying between them, Aneka's shrill screams floating back above the drumming hooves. I finally got control of Dester and turned him after the litter, at a less breakneck pace—nothing excites a runaway like being chased. Then a last mutter and rumble came above me, and another few boulders crashed down. I think a pebble or something got Dester on the quarters, because he squealed again, and leapt forward: I stayed on by some miracle, and found I was clinging to the pommel while he went down the road after the litter as if there were wings on his big feet.

I still don't know where we went. After the litter, yes, but that left the road soon. I was too busy staying on and trying to get control to look at the scenery. When Dester tired I finally got control, and drove him on at the trot although he wanted to stop and get his breath back. We were on a track, and up ahead was the litter, on a sort of knoll beyond an overhang: it was intact and securely fastened to both horses, who stood with heads down, sides heaving. Aneka was still moaning inside it. I was concentrating on that, which is why the man who jumped me from the overhang took me quite by surprise. I marked him, with teeth and nails, and I had nearly got the upper hand when his companion came running up and struck me over the head. Sparks flared, and I fell into night.

I woke in torchlight. It flickered and leapt beyond my closed eyelids, and above the crackle of the pine were small sounds, rustling and breathing. My head hurt: I wondered vaguely why, and then remembered—

"Aneka?" I said, opening my eyes. She appeared beside me, looking only relieved, though the tearstains still showed.

"Does it hurt?" she said. "Your head."

I put up my hand and felt gingerly. A lump where the neck muscles join the skull stabbed pain when I touched it. No blood.

"I'll live," I said. "Where are we? What happened?"

"I don't know," she said. "Thula, I'm frightened!"

"Tell me what happened after I was laid out." I suggested, and sat up with caution. I was on a high, well-draped bed: about us were kists and a cupboard, and a curtain that swung in the draught and probably covered a garde-robe. The window was shuttered: a high fireplace gaped blackly across the room. "How did we get here?" I prodded. She sat on the bed beside me.

"They threw you in on top of me," she said obediently. "They wouldn't speak to me, I don't understand what they said to each other. I didn't see where we went, I was trying to wake you. Then they made me get out in the courtyard here and two of them carried you, and one took my arm, and we came here. And I couldn't wake you. So I went to sleep," she finished.

That made me giggle. It hurt, so I stopped abruptly: Aneka gave me a dignified look and added, "There's some food."

With a glass of wine and a chicken wing I felt better. I prowled round the room eating, relieved to find my legs would bear me. I could see no way out. I kept remembering the words of Aneka's lover: *If you do not come to me by your will, you shall come by mine.* What could I do, with Aneka to take care of? I had to get her to her husband in Maer-Cuith, but how should we escape from here?

The door flung open. Aneka drew breath as if to scream: I reached for my dagger, but the second man had a crossbow, wound and loaded and pointing at me. The first bowed to Aneka and took her wrist: the second stood aside into the room: the third came in and took my arm, and he had a knife in his other hand. Aneka said "Thula—!"

"It's all right," I said. "I don't think they're going to hurt you."

We were led down the wheel stair, the crossbow at the

back of my neck. At the foot of the stair a boy with a torch bobbed and stared at Aneka, then turned and went off along a corridor, into the deeps of the castle. We were led after, our escorts never letting go, the crossbower padding softly behind me on felt-soled boots. Through many corridors we went, and up more stairs, till I began to think of rabbit-warrens. Then we halted at a door. Aneka's guide knocked and spoke harshly. The door was opened, and we stepped into a glare of torches and candles. Aneka stood in front of me maybe three seconds: then she gave a great cry of "Fenist! Oh, Fenist!" She ran forward, and I was prodded into the room. The door closed.

And in front of me Aneka knelt by a bed heaped with furs. The light of many candles fell on her head, and on the hand that came from among the furs and lay on her neck like a caress. I walked round the bed, the crossbow following as I moved, until I could see her face. She was bent over the man in the bed, kissing him quickly with light practised movements. He was whispering, the words half lost against her face, over and over: "Aneka, my dear love, my heart's delight, Aneka . . ."

I watched with the half-dozen men in the room, for some time. At length I stepped forward, despite the insistent crossbow at my side, and put my hand on her shoulder. She looked round, startled, and the man's eyes rose to mine. I looked away from the challenge in them, and said gently,

"Aneka, you're promised. Remember? You're betrothed to Alevr ma Julden of Dervir—"

"I made no promises!" she said. "I signed no contracts. Women are not chattels, Thula, to be bargained for like diamonds and cinnamon, you should know that!"

"She is mine," said the man among the furs. I straightened, and this time met his hawk's eyes squarely.

"Goodsir, I swore a convenant with her father, that she would reach her husband's house as she left her father's, or not at all. I swore to defend her honour as my own. My honour is a small thing—" His eyes mocked me and I added hastily, "except to me, but the Order loses twenty crescents and honour as well."

"I'll give you forty," he said. The eyes danced: under his beaked nose the cruel mouth suddenly smiled entrancingly. "There is the matter that she hasn't reached me as she left her father's house, but I'll forget that in the circumstances."

"I should kill her," I said. At my feet Aneka shrank into the crook of her lover's arm.

"And how far would you go from here if you did?" He was watching me with a certain amount of sympathy. "Mistress, how would her life be in the women's quarters of Alevr ma Julden's house?"

I remembered, dimly, my mother's life, before I was given to the Order. Scents and rustling gowns, other ladies coming and going, and the echo of my father's voice making her freeze like a rabbit hearing a fox. The man was watching me.

"Just so," he said, reading my expression. "Here she will be mistress of my castle and councilor of my people. I may even teach her to read." He kissed the end of her nose, and turned back to stare at me, like a hawk hovering, for a long moment. Then the hawk swooped.

"I'm damned if I'll lie here," he said moving stiffly among the furs, "helping you argue down your conscience. Obik, fetch me the board yonder! Mistress, I'll play you three games of Siege. If I win three, Aneka decides your fate and hers. If I win two, you may go free and no more said. If you win two, you may try if you can persuade Aneka to go with you."

"And if I win three?" I said. He laughed, and winced as if it hurt him.

"You won't," he said confidently.

"But *you* will, love," said Aneka. "I beat her last night, and you can beat me."

He kissed her again, and brought the other arm out of the furs to wave me to a seat across the board. White linen on the brown skin made Aneka gasp.

"Oh, Fenist, I thought—" She looked at his arm, and then pulled back the furs. More linen was swathed about his belly where the ribs stopped. She stared for a moment, then tucked the furs round him again and raised her eyes to my face.

"You did that," she said. I knew suddenly that it would not be good to lose three games. And I had thought she liked me . . .

"In the line of duty," said Fenist. "I bear no grudges.

I was foolish, perhaps." He inspected the pieces laid out
on the board. "My move to start, mistress? So—King's
Captain, advance three paces."

I looked up, startled, but he had turned back to Aneka.
That move opened the most famous of the ritual games,
and was rarely used otherwise. Perhaps I was imagining
things . . . ? I replied with the following move— King's
Captain to the corner turret. He looked back at the click
of the piece on the board, and moved his Queen's Soldier
two squares left without hesitating. Across the squared
board his eyes met mine, unreadable: when I made pre-
tence to consider before moving the Queen's Knight in
support of my King's Captain, he smiled gently, and
shifted carefully among the furs. I stared at the board,
not seeing it. This was ritual play, and I was to win.
Why?

"So I go free," I said, setting up the pieces for the
second game. He smiled again, and nodded.

"So you go free, mistress. Your move to start."

I hesitated, hand over the board. If I won, I could try
to persuade Aneka to leave, and honour her father's
promise. If I lost I might still win the next one. I lifted
my Queen, still hesitating. If she merely moved in support of her King, set at the front of the siege from the
beginning, that was an ambiguous start. But if she moved
to the attack . . .

"So," I said. "Queen to the corner turret."

His smile showed that he appreciated the move.

"Very symbolic," he said. "So is my move. King to
the corner turret."

A cold finger stroked my backbone. This was free
play, and I was playing with either a master or a fool.
Somehow, looking at the narrow, intent face, I could not
think the Lord Fenist a fool. But they teach us well, in
the Order, before they send us out in the world. I moved
my King to support my Queen.

This game took longer. Aneka and his soldiers watched
in silence, unmoving. We two did not stir, except to reach
over the board, moving the ebony and ivory pieces. The
only sound was the click of the men on the board and the
hiss and crackle of the torches on the wall, and the slow
breathing of my opponent.

"Mate," he said at last. "In three moves, not so?"

"Five," I said.

"Well, five," he conceded reluctantly. "Obik! Wine for the ladies."

I stretched, and realised my head was aching. He watched me, the cruel mouth smiling under his hawk's beak of a nose.

"Will you not admit me the third game?" he said. "Admit you are outplayed?"

I had been considering doing just that.

"No," I said. He laughed, and winced. I drank wine, and set up the pieces. "You lose a man," I said. "I defend, so you move first."

He considered a moment. Then he moved—King's Soldier right three paces. Another opening rarely used outside the rituals, and this time he was to win. I looked at the board, and then at him. The next move to this game was Queen's Soldier to the rampart, two paces. I considered for more than a moment; then I lifted my Queen.

"Queen to the corner turret," I said clearly, and set her down. His hand had been hovering already over his Queen's Soldier, to move it in support of the other piece; at my words he looked back sharply from Aneka's up-turned face. One comprehensive glance and he began laughing, his hand to his side.

"Oh, don't, love—!" said Aneka anxiously. "Fenist, please don't, you'll make it bleed!"

"I know," he said, still laughing weakly. "Oh, you show your teeth, mistress! Well here is your answer. King to the corner turret."

That game took longest of the three. Aneka and the soldiers watched in silence; the only sounds were the click of the men on the ebony and ivory board, and the hiss and crackle of the torches, and the slow breathing of my opponent. It took the longest, and it was won by the least margin.

"Mate," he said at length. "In three moves, with these three men. King's Captain moves there, this soldier here, this one here, and I hold the castle."

"I can see," I said. "No need to spell it out. Falcon's Mate."

"No," he said, frowning. "No need." He lay back among the furs, grey-faced. I stood up, saying,

"Goodsir, when do I go free?"

"In the morning," he said. "I'll give you food, and a spare horse." His speech was slurred; Aneka, bending hastily over him, was the only one who caught his next words, before he slid into sleep. She straightened; across the bed piled with furs her eyes met mine, unloving.

"You lose hard," she repeated. She looked round at the men. "Go house her as my lord would wish," she said. "The place we were in will do."

I turned at the door, despite the crossbow once more insistent at my shoulder.

"Aneka," I said. She was still watching me. "What does it say on my sword?"

She stared at me, remembering slowly.

"A friend has two edges," she said at last. There was another silence; then she crossed the room. The bower stood aside for her, and she leaned up and kissed my cheek, and then turned back to her sleeping lord.

"Goodnight, Aneka," I said.

"Goodbye, my friend," she said. "It's nearly dawn."

So I rode alone, down from the Old Mountains into Amyn on the road south-west, with forty gold crescents close packed in one saddle-bag as Aneka's bride price, and ten in the other as my wages, since it would be unwise to try to collect from Alevr ma Julden. And my conscience was unquiet, for the game of Siege, sacred to the Moon, should not be used as I had used it. The difference is subtle, between one losing and another winning, and whatever he might think, Lord Fenist, Fenist the Falcon, had not won the last game. I had lost it. There are many more games written down than are ever used in the rituals.

Charles R. Saunders

THE CITY OF MADNESS

The fanzines are proving themselves to be a fertile source for new stories by new writers. This yarn, for instance, I found in a fanzine called Dark Fantasy. *In it, Charles Saunders does something so original and so ingenious and yet so obvious, that it surprises me that no one ever thought of it before (in fact, I wish I'd thought of it myself!): he combines the vivid, swashbuckling heroica of Howard's Conan with the jungle scenery, savage character and even the native names for beasts you find in Burroughs' Tarzan. What makes this such an exciting find is not only that Saunders is a brand new writer, but this happens to be the very first story he's ever written! I venture to predict we will be hearing a lot from him in the years to come.*

—LC

1. THE SCARLET DEATH

Rudely shattered was the daylit silence of the green brooding forest. Birds fled through the upper terraces of leaves in screeching explosions, and long-tailed monkeys scampered excitedly from branch to branch, chattering and scolding in alarm. Even the fiercest of the jungle predators paused uncertainly in their hunting as the alien and unfamiliar thing which had caused this disturbance drew nearer. They were strange, these sounds, as if some beast mightier than any of those who dwelt within the jungle now had intruded upon its verdant stillness.

The mysterious intruder, the beasts somehow sensed, was unlike the two strangers who had come this way but recently.

Here in this calm glade, the trees were set far apart and a bit further on, many such clearings were to be found. Now there stepped forth into the clear sunlight of the open glade the creature who had been the cause of the strange sounds the beasts had paused to ponder suspiciously. *Man!* It was Man, the unwelcome intruder into this hitherto untouched and primal domain. And now the nature of those curious and alien sounds could also be discerned, for as he advanced, the intruder slashed and hacked a path through the dense foliage which bordered the clearing, brandishing a great, glittering scimitar of blue Azanian steel.

As he stepped into the clearing, the man bent down, his glance darting searchingly along the leaf-littered ground. With a grunt of satisfaction, he straightened, revealing his giant stature.

Massive yet lithe was his half-naked physique, with wide shoulders, broad chest, narrow, sinewy waist, and long, muscular legs. Smooth dark-cocoa skin gleamed with the sheen of sweat through tattered clothing that hung in scanty rags upon his huge frame. Blood-crusted wounds stood out like red runes against his dark skin, and his wooly hair was matted with dried gore.

At another time, his face might have been considered handsome in a rough way. It had the aspect of a young man who had but recently left adolescence and entered his prime. But the thick, full lips, the short, wide-flaring nose, and deep-set obsidian eyes were frozen into an implacable mask of hatred. Devil-lights of fierce vengeance and bloodstained broodings flickered in those terrible eyes; perhaps this was why the forest creatures fled his approach.

One, however, did not flee. Even now this one was stalking soundlessly closer to the young black giant, using a leaf-shrouded limb as its avenue of approach.

Oblivious to the lurking death was the grim warrior. So intent was he upon following the latest spoor of those whom he pursued that he was nearly undone by the silent pounce of Death from the high trees. Only primal instinct and lightning-like reflexes enabled him to hurl himself aside in time. Even so, one shoulder was raked by long lethal talons as the tree-beast narrowly missed its target.

Instantly the young warrior regained his feet and whirled to face his foe. Snarling hideously in rage and frustration was Chui Nyekundu, the red panther, one of the most feared predators in all Nyumbani. Halfway between a leopard and a lioness in size, Chui Nyekundu was leanly and compactly built. Fearsome weapons were its claws, but far more dangerous were the long sabre-fangs that hooked below its tufted chin. The solid, blood-red hue of its fur was the source of Chui Nyekundu's name.

Like a crimson flash, the great cat sprang again, its slavering mouth agape so that it could drive its deadly fangs deep into the warrior's throat. And again, incredibly, the black man eluded its attack. This time he leaped onto the beast's back as its momentum carried it past him. His sword discarded, the warrior whipped out a dagger and plunged it into Chui Nyekundu's side.

For a brief moment, the panther lay pinned to earth by the young giant's weight. But when the blade struck, Chui Nyekundu squalled in pain, and leaped furiously about the forest floor as though the warrior's weight was nothing. The human clung tenaciously, legs locked vise-like around the great cat's body, arms out of the reach of the deadly fangs.

Again and again the dagger bit deep into the flesh of Chui Nyekundu, until the red fur was spattered with the brighter scarlet of its own blood. Slowly its savage struggles diminished. Its screaming snarls diminished. Then the black warrior's blade found Chui Nyekundu's heart.

One final convulsion; then the red panther was still. The warrior stood up and looked down at his dead adversary. Born in the wide yellow plain south of Lake Nyanza, he had never before encountered this dreaded killer of the woodlands. Still, he had triumphed, just as

he had conquered Mkara the lion to pass his tribe's test
of manhood. ...

Breathing heavily from his exertions, the black man
grimaced ruefully as he wiped the beast-gore from the
blade of his dagger. As he retrieved his sword, he reflected on the fact that he had but narrowly escaped
becoming Chui Nyekundu's next dinner. Obviously he
would have to pay more attention to woodcraft if he
meant to survive.

Despite that, the trail of those whom he was pursuing
was easy to follow. They had no more woodcraft than
he. Warier and wiser, the warrior continued his grim
pursuit.

2.   BLACK SKULLS

After an hour of slashing his way through the foliage,
the warrior's sharp ears caught faint sounds that were
unmistakably human voices. His heart leaped in savage
joy. At last his prey was near! The thought kindled feral
fires in his eyes ...

As he drew closer, the warrior's brow furrowed in
puzzlement. For they were speaking in a language unfamiliar to his ear. Moreover, the speech was punctuated
by bursts of harsh laughter and loud yelps of pain.

Though his mind was consumed with his mission of
revenge, the warrior was still curious enough to investi-
gate the strange sounds. He could see that the source of
the voices was in the path of the trail of his quarry.
Whatever the connection was, he intended to find it.

Stealthily as Chui Nyekundu himself, he came to the
last barrier of brush. Drawing aside the thorny under-
growth, he stared wide-eyed at what was revealed.

Four men stood in the clearing. None of them re-
sembled any of the races familiar to the hidden warrior.
Three of them were complete anomalies: men of medium
stature with unnaturally light skins, narrow features, and
snakelike black locks curling downward from rusty metal
helmets. Armor of worn leather and dented metal plates
protected their bodies.

Strange and weird were the ornaments around their lean waists. Each of the three armored men wore a human skull dangling from a golden chain. The skulls were painted black.

Evil glee was etched upon the faces of the three, for they were having sport with the fourth man, who was the most unusual looking of them all.

He was no bigger than a dwarf, but perfectly proportioned. His naked body was reddish brown in color, and bled profusely in several places, notably the buttocks. This was the spot in which the bigger men were jabbing him with their slender swords. Whenever the pygmy desperately attempted to evade the poking swordpoints, the pale men kicked him viciously.

The still-hidden warrior did not like what he saw. Something about the appearance of the light-skinned torturers stirred a loathing that crept unbidden from the deepest recesses of his memory. Also, the plight of the diminutive, helpless victim touched his sense of compassion.

Whatever his motivations, the warrior wasted no further time contemplating them. Sweeping aside the thornbush with one great arm, he charged into the clearing, voicing the terrifying war cry of his people. The three men were shocked into momentary inaction by that cry. Sounding halfway between the roar of Nunda the sabre-tooth and the scream of Koddoleo the baboon, it had demoralized the people of the eastern plains for generations.

In a silvery arc of death, the warrior's blade sheared through the neck of his nearest adversary. Before he could even scream, his helmeted head flew in one direction as his blood-fountaining body in the other. With blurring speed, the warrior turned and thrust his sword into the second foeman's belly. Its point tore through his back. One gurgling shriek, then the pale man's mouth gushed crimson and was still.

In the time it took the ebon giant to wrench his weapon free from the corpse, the third man had recovered sufficient poise to defend himself. The effort was pitiful. Despite his advantages of armor and longer sword, his movements were awkward and unskilled. Also, his fear of this frightful black apparition had dampened his desire for combat.

The giant did not even bother to toy with his last opponent. Three savage blows from his mighty arm, and the pale man joined his companions in the Death Hell of Mashataan. He lay face down in a widening pool of blood, his sword broken and his head split from crown to nape.

As the warrior wiped his sword-blade on the garments of the fallen, the pygmy looked warily up at him. The sudden, irresistible onslaught of this giant caused him apprehension. Was he really safe now? Or had he gone from the jaws of the jackal to the maw of the crocodile?

The fierce-faced warrior stared silently and impassively at the tiny man before him. At first he had thought him a member of the Iwa, a furtive little folk who haunted the misty outlands of the cruel kingdom of Rwanda. But this one was even shorter than they, and his childlike features and bulbous forehead were unlike the Iwa or anyone else he had ever seen.

Marking that the small one remained uneasy, the warrior spoke to him in *ngwana,* a lingua franca of Nyumbani.

"Yambo, stranger," he said in a rumbling, barbaric accent. "I be Imaro, formerly of the tribe of Ilyassai. Strange are the ways of the Gods, that we should meet in blood-bond in this strange and unknown land."

The pygmy sighed in deep relief. The warrior had given the proper greeting of the Old Codes, and acknowledged that in the act of saving his life a mutual obligation had been established.

"Yambo-kuu, warrior," he replied. "I am Pomphis, once of the Bambuti, now of Cush. My life is yours, and yours is mine."

With the formalities done with, Imaro said, "All right little man, let's take a look at those pinpricks in your backside."

"The name is *Pomphis!*" fumed Pomphis as the giant bent to inspect his slight wounds.

3.   DEFEAT AND BETRAYAL

Pomphis' pique did not last long. After his wounds had been tended, and he had recovered his dignity along with his fine linen garments, he began to regale Imaro with the story of his life. Naturally garrulous, Pomphis pretended not to notice that Imaro's attention often appeared to be elsewhere.

Pomphis was a Bambuti, the ancient, half-mythical race of pygmies who dwelt in the Ituri Kubwa, that vast rain forest far to the west. As a child, he and his band had ventured too close to the edge of their jungle world, and had been captured by a crew of Komeh slave raiders. One by one, the adult Bambuti had died. For there is no more certain way to kill a Bambuti than to remove him from his forest home.

However, no one had bothered to inform young Pomphis of this. Thus, only he had survived the long trek eastward.

In the market of Malindi, jewel-spired capital of Azania, the pygmy had brought his captors a high price as a curiosity. For years, he had lived a degrading existence as a *mjimja*—a jester in the court of the Shaa.

The life of the little *mjimja* fell into danger when he was caught in bed with one of the Shaa's nubile young daughters. At the moment of his imminent (and highly painful) execution, the pygmy's life was saved from an unexpected source.

It seemed that a man named Khabatekh of the High Empire of Cush was interested in purchasing the *mjimja* for purposes of scientific investigation. The Shaa grudgingly agreed. He knew better than to affront a scholar-sorceror of Cush, that incredibly ancient and powerful northern civilization.

Thus did the Bambuti depart from Malindi. The Shaa ground his teeth in rage at his ex-mjimja's parting comment that he hoped he had sired a new dynasty of four-foot-tall rulers for the kingdom!

Initially ecstatic at the opportunity to study a live

Bambuti, Khabatekh was disappointed to discover that his subject had forgotten most of his childhood existence in the Ituri Kubwa. He couldn't even recall the name that his long-dead parents had bestowed upon him.

Nevertheless, the Cushite had taken a liking to the quick-witted pygmy, a circumstance doubtlessly enhanced by the latter's decided reluctance to be returned to the court of the Shaa . . .

Eventually, Khabatekh had adopted the pygmy as his assistant and protégé, and gave him both his freedom and the name "Pomphis," which was High Cushite for "Know-it-all." Together, Pomphis and Khabatekh had made the long voyage northward to the fabulous realm of Cush. There, Pomphis had seen many marvels and wonders: the colossal purple pyramids, the beautiful golden-spired cities, the domesticated black lions, and the enigmatic people with their brown skins, bushy hair, and alien yellow eyes. The Cushites claimed descent from the Mtembi ya Mbinguni, the Gods of the continent of Nyumbani. However, Pomphis had found the women human enough.

Khabatekh still found time to impart to Pomphis a sizeable fraction of his voluminous and arcane knowledge, and the pygmy had proved to be an apt and diligent pupil.

Khabatekh succumbed at length to wanderlust: he and Pomphis had set off for the wild hills south of Punt and Axum. The trip ended in tragic disaster. They were attacked by a band of brigands, and before he could unleash any protective sorcery, Khabatekh was slain. Pomphis had managed to escape the outlaws, and had eventually sought refuge in the forest far from the hills.

"It was fortunate for me," Pomphis concluded, "that Khabatekh, who was like a father to me, taught me how to survive in the forest. Ironic, isn't it, that a citizen of the oldest civilization in Nyumbani should have to instruct a Bambuti in woodcraft!"

After an interval of somewhat strained silence, Pomphis asked Imaro, "And what brought you, warrior, to this nameless locale—fortunately for me, of course?"

Imaro had fallen captive to the Mwambututssi, the cruel Overlords of the kingdom of Rwanda, and was enslaved to labor in their mines. An Ilyassai, however, did not submit easily to slavery. Before a month had passed,

Imaro was free, having led a revolt of the slaves. The revolt's success had been due as much to the phenomenal strength and courage of its leader as to the sudden intervention of a bandit horde led by a redoubtable outlaw named Rumanzila the Ravager. Rumanzila had taken full advantage of the chaos caused by Imaro's revolt to loot the Mwambututssi's gold.

In the confusion and slaughter, Imaro and Rumanzila struck a bloodsoaked bargain. The ex-slaves would join Rumanzila's desperadoes. There was enough captured gold and other booty to satisfy all the men. And there was the lure of more to come. The newly combined force was formidable enough to pose a threat to the whole kingdom of Rwanda.

With his share of the loot, Imaro had also taken Tanisha, a Kahutu girl who had been the mistress of the overseer of the mine. Imaro had killed him with his bare hands. And he had vowed to do the same to anyone who dared to touch the woman he claimed for his own . . .

Inevitably, dissension had arisen among this motley crew of cutthroats. There wouldn't have been enough room in an empire, let alone an outlaw gang, for two leaders the stature of Imaro and Rumanzila. A petty difference of opinion had erupted into a duel to the death. Imaro had emerged bloody but victorious, his strength and skill overcoming the older man's cunning and experience. None dared dispute Imaro's claim to the leadership of the band. None, that is, until Bomunu, a shrewd exile from the coastal kingdom of Zanj, began to cast covetous eyes upon the voluptuous form of Tanisha . . .

Imaro was not a strategist, but his reckless daring made up for that. Soon his savage raids became the scourge of Rwanda, Ulindu, and even the borderlands of mighty Azania. Armies sent out to destroy the outlaws were scattered and decimated. It was the treachery of Bomunu that spelled the downfall of Imaro's rising star.

Furtively, the man of Zanj had contacted Rwanda and Azania, and conspired to sell the lives of his comrades. As a trusted lieutenant, Bomunu was in an ideal position to do so.

On a pretext, Bomunu had led the rest of the outlaws into the jaws of a deadly trap. In a blind valley near the

swift Kakassa River, they were cut to pieces by a superior
force of Azanian and Rwandan troops.

As arranged, Bomunu escaped with a sack of Azanian
diamonds under one arm and Tanisha under the other. He
headed for the Soudanic Kingdoms of the west, and
wealthy oblivion. There was a hitch in his plans, however.
Of all the five thousand bandits that had fought by the
Kakassa, one had survived: Imaro.

The Ilyassai had managed to escape the massacre before the field was overrun with vultures and hyenas. His
heart heavy with the deaths of men who had trusted him,
and burning with hatred for the traitor Bomunu, Imaro
set out on the trail of the betrayer who had stolen his
woman. He had followed them across the hills of Rwanda,
and into this forest where he had encountered Pomphis
and his tormenters.

"And I will continue my pursuit," Imaro said grimly,
"Until I catch up with them. Then will vengeance be
mine."

Looking into the barbarian's black gaze, Pomphis was
hesitant to tell him what he had seen before his capture.
This man was a reaver and a bandit, like the men who
killed Khabatekh. But he had saved Pomphis' life!

Pomphis drew himself up to his full four-foot-six-inch
height, and said, "I think I can help you."

"You've seen them?" he demanded. "Where are they?
Tell me, damn you!"

A practised twist extricated Pomphis from Imaro's
grasp.

"Have a care, warrior," he said calmly. "I shall tell
you what I know of those you seek. But there is no need
to lay hands on me."

Imaro's passion subsided, although his fists continued
to open and close. His silence was his apology.

Then Pomphis related how he had seen a tall, sly-
faced man and a wide-hipped woman captured by pale,
armored strangers similar to those lying dead in the clearing. They had gone in a westerly direction.

"The trail is fresh," said Pomphis, "we should be able
to follow it without much trouble."

Imaro noted that the pygmy had said "We." But his
only comment was, "Good. Let's get going."

As he cast a last glance at the sprawled corpses, already crawling with flies, Imaro observed, "I've never seen men like those before. What do you think they are?"

"From the look of them," Pomphis answered thoughtfully, "I would think that they are Mizungus of Atlantis. But they were driven out of Nyumbani centuries ago."

Mizungus! Atlantis! In a flash of half-memory, Imaro recognized the source of the unconscious loathing he had felt for the pale skull-wearers . . . Though the cataclysmic war between the white men of Atlantis and the black men of Nyumbani had ended a thousand years ago, the wounds it had inflicted still ran red. Images of the conflict crowded rapidly into his mind. He saw the triumph of the Mashataan over the Sky Walkers; the invasion of the white demon-hordes from across the Western Sea; cruel Atlanteans and their barbarian allies from Thule laid waste to the West Coast, ravaged the Jungle Kingdoms south of Otongi, and crossed the Ataissan Mountains to wreak havoc upon the vast grasslands. Though the men of Nyumbani had fought bravely and mightily, the terrifying war beasts and magical weapons of the Atlanteans had given them a seemingly insurmountable advantage.

Then the Cushites had discovered a way to summon the Sky Walkers. These titans had hurled the Mashataan out of the dimensional plane of Earth, thus nullifying the power of the Mizungus' eldritch devices. Nyumbani had united and in a series of battles, drove the Mizungus back across the sea to Atlantis. Those left behind were slain without mercy, remembering the atrocities they had committed upon the people of Nyumbani.

Some had escaped the slaughter and found refuge in the most inaccessible corners of the black continent. Imaro and Pomphis assumed that the pale, armored men who inhabited this forest were surviving Mizungus. But their reactions to this were different.

Pomphis was merely curious. Under the tutelege of Khabatekh, he had studied the history of the Mizungu War, and had learned that the Atlanteans had been duped into the attack by a false priesthood corrupted by the Mashataan. Pomphis wondered to what extent these surviving Mizungus had retained their tragic delusions.

Imaro knew nothing of the Cushite histories of the

War. His knowledge came from tales passed down in simplified, distorted form, told in whispers around flickering night-fires. To him, Mizungus were Mizungus: devils of Atlantis, to be abhorred but less than the Mashataan themselves.

Imaro growled: "Others of their kind may be searching for these dogs right now. We should get out of here quickly."

"I agree," said Pomphis. "These Mizungus must dwell somewhere close to here, and it is probably there that Tanisha and Bomunu were taken."

Imaro agreed. "We will follow them even if their trail leads past Motoni itself!"

Pomphis rolled his eyes skyward. He was obligated by the Old Codes to go along with this oversized madman, even if they did have to go to Motoni, that immense chain of volcanoes at the northern extreme of the continent.

"In my reading of the Chronicles of Nabatti," Pomphis mused, "I came across dim legends of a city of Atlantis that somehow survived over the centuries, 'M'ji Ya Wazimu,' it was called. 'The City of Madness.' I wonder if those legends are true?"

"We'll find out soon enough," grunted Imaro.

4. THE BROKEN CITY

In the white glare of moonlight, the dark city brooded like some vast behemoth of the night. But the two figures stealthily approaching its portal had seen how the city looked in full daylight. They knew that it was nothing more than a dead ruin, inhabited by the remnants of a dying people. Imaro and Pomphis had seen the cracked walls and the broken pylons of Atlantean architecture.

Also, they had seen Bomunu. Or at least what was left of him . . . Never would Imaro gain the vengeance he had sought against the traitor. Bomunu's headless corpse hung impaled upon an iron spike, the gory, pointed end of which protruded through his neck as a macabre replacement for his absent head. Torture had so mutilated the body that only the embossed Zanjian belt told Imaro that this bloody thing had indeed once been Bomunu. As to his missing head, the pair uneasily recalled the painted skulls that hung from the waists of the Mizungu warriors . . .

Imaro was reasonably certain that Tanisha was alive inside the decaying city. From what he knew of Mizungu culture, Pomphis agreed. As the two laid plans for slipping into the city, Pomphis wondered at the ever-changing moods of his tall companion. Had he been the raving wild man of earlier that day, Imaro might have attempted to storm the ruined city single-handed. Now, the Bambuti was mildly surprised by the Ilyassai's level-headed suggestions. He could see how this man could have welded together a collection of cutthroats and thieves into a formidable army of brigands.

The lone guard at the crumbling wall was not diligent. His duties were of only token significance, since the beasts shunned his city, and his people did not fear other men. Shifting to a more comfortable position he longed to join in the rites that were now commencing. Decades had passed since black men had last set foot in the Atlanteans' hidden domain. Of those who had been captured today, the man hung impaled outside the gate, and the woman was part of the ceremony inside. So engrossed were the Mizungus in their rituals that they were not curious about three soldiers who had failed to return.

A sudden sound behind him woke the guard from his reverie. Whirling, he attempted to draw his sword. But his reaction was too slow and too late. A brawny forearm clamped like an iron bar across his throat; steely fingers held his sword arm immobile.

The guard was a big man, but for all his violent struggles, he was held like a child in the relentless grasp of his unseen assailant. As the massive forearm crushed his windpipe, the guard tried to shriek a warning. But the only sound he could make was a gurgle. Before death blackened his vision, the Mizungu dimly discerned a man the size of a child grinning up at him, teeth flashing whitely in the moonlight.

Because the guard was almost as large as Imaro, his armor and helmet fit the barbarian tightly but adequately. Thus disguised, he strode swiftly down the weed-choked street of the city, following the drumbeats and the sound of weird chanting. Beside him, Pomphis slipped like a wraith between the grotesque shadows cast by broken buildings. Imaro was careful to keep his eyes from lingering overlong upon the sculptures and inscriptions lining the rotting walls lest they ensorcel his mind.

Imaro and Pomphis were drawn down the ancient avenue to the source from which the strange sounds came. It was a cube-shaped edifice in better condition than the rest of the city's buildings. In fact, it looked completely untouched by the breath of Time. Like a guardian of the destiny of its people, the titanic structure squatted in the center of the ruined city.

As they padded noiselessly up the steps to the yawning entrance to the mysterious edifice, the two observed it was windowless, and its granite face was covered with intricate bas-reliefs depicting scenes of unspeakable and obscene cruelty. Imaro ground his teeth at the thought of the suffering of the unfortunates who must have been dragged screaming into this malignant temple when this City of Madness was first built. Pomphis sadly reflected that the Mizungus had not forsworn the sins of their ancestors.

They saw that the entrance was guarded by nothing other than the pair of sculptured stone serpent-things whose long necks formed a forbidding archway.

They peered down a long dark hall cut out of solid stone, and saw at its end a square of lurid, unsteady light. This light then, was their destination. Like hunting panthers, Imaro and Pomphis stalked toward it.

5.   *HORROR ENTHRONED*

Concealed by wavering shadows, Pomphis and Imaro stared at what must have been the entire population of the ruined city participating in a ceremony of ominous splendor. The celebrants were men, and they were naked except for the ever-present black skulls dangling upon their loins. To the rhythmic beat of drums, the Mizungus capered and cavorted in peculiar fashion, shouting and screaming in meaningless words.

Though they may once have been a comely race, now the Mizungus bore the marks of advanced dissipation. Loose, raddled flesh swayed and jiggled on their bodies. All of them wore loose-lipped, intoxicated expressions on their pale faces, as though they had been inhaling the fumes of the swamp lotus.

The attention of Imaro and Pomphis was held not by the orgiastic throng, but on that which lay at the center of the temple chamber.

A colossal throne sat behind a high altar. Upon the throne hunkered an image of revolting ugliness. Carved from pitted, unidentifiable gray-green rock, it was a statue of one of the most loathesome of the Mashataan—an Azuth!

At first it looked like some monstrous kind of ape. From the waist up, the Azuth was indeed gorilloid in aspect, though its wide mouth sprouted tusks that would have been envied by even Nunda the sabre-tooth. But from the waist down it had the legs of a goat, with sharp, lethal hooves in place of feet.

Creations of the Mashataan, Azuths had menaced mankind eons ago until Thutanas, a scientist of Cush, bred the famous black lions which were more than a match for the Azuths. Supposedly the ape-things had been driven from Cush long ago. But even though the thing on the throne was only a stone image, it seemed to be leering with empty eyes at the altar before it.

Upon the polished altar lay Tanisha. Arms and legs bound in a spread-eagle position, her nude black body was an aesthetic contrast to the Mizungus. She had lush feminine proportions, and an attractive face framed by a circle of kinky black hair. The firm, dark globes of her breasts thrust as she breathed in labored gasps. Her frantic brown eyes darted about as her ordeal approached its climax. Hopelessly twisting her supple body from side to side, Tanisha awaited her doom—

Leaping and prancing around Tanisha's altar was the high priest of the Azuth. He looked no different than his fellow Minzungus, save that he was taller and had eight black-painted skulls encircling his flabby waist—and a freshly painted one cradled in both gnarled hands.

Suddenly the priest dropped to his bony knees. Waving the black skull in a slow circle, he began to harangue the stone image of the Azuth, invoking names whose alien syllables made Imaro's skin crawl in disgust.

Sensing that the time had come to put their plan into action, Imaro poked Pomphis with an impatient elbow.

As if propelled from a catapult, Pomphis hurtled into the torchlit chamber. In a voice loud and deep, the pygmy bellowed imprecations in the same guttural tongue that the Mizungus were using. The effects of Pomphis' speech were instantaneous—and remarkable.

Ceasing their awkward gyrations, the entire assemblage of Atlanteans stood stock-still and goggle-eyed for a long, frozen moment. Then they broke into an hysterical frenzy, shrieking, in inchoate rage. Froth flying from their distended mouths, the Mizungus looked wildly about, seeking the utterer of blasphemy.

With a wicked grin on his childlike face, Pomphis repeated the inflammatory phrase in even louder tones. Now he caught the eye of the Mizungus. As one, they rushed at the Bambuti, despite the imprecations of their priest. Pomphis turned on his heel and fled down the dark corridor, showing a speed that was not surprising considering the circumstances.

Imaro flattened himself against the wall. Just as Pomphis had predicted, between the blending of Imaro's skin into the darkness and the Mizungus' single-minded, murderous pursuit, the screaming mob rushed by without noticing him.

He waited until the last footsteps had faded out of the temple. Then the massive Ilyassai entered the chamber.

6. WHEN HORROR WALKS

The priest lifted his head at this new intrusion. He stared in incredulity. Despite the Atlantean armor he was wearing, the giant's arms and legs were too black to belong to one of his people. Tanisha, bound to the Azuth's altar, failed to recognize Imaro.

Knowing that he had no chance against the black

giant, the cunning priest had only one chance: to complete the ceremony. He had mere seconds to do so. With lightening speed, the priest heaved the fresh black skull directly at the squatting statue of the Azuth, which produced singular results.

For the skull literally exploded upon contact with the stone surface of the Azuth, splintered bits flying in all directions.

This stopped Imaro in his tracks. As he stared in disbelief, a filmy substance began to emerge from the shattered remnants of the black skull. The smoky, translucent substance eerily coalesced into an unstable human figure with flaming slits of eyes that glared directly into those of Imaro. Gradually, inexorably, the ghost-thing began to merge with the stone image of the Azuth. And as the shadow-substance was absorbed into the idol, a horrible transmutation took place. The gray-green stone was becoming living, breathing flesh.

In a flash Imaro understood. Nameless terrors began to claw insistently at him, threatening to unman the mighty warrior. Only to one person could this fresh, new skull belong. To only one man could Imaro attribute the malevolent eyes of the smoky wraith-thing. The vague, misty figure, now completely absorbed into the statue of the Azuth, could only be the *n'kaa,* the death-spirit, of his foe, Bomunu. The priest had freed Bomunu's *n'kaa* from its spell-made prison. And the fury of the lost soul that now animated the living Azuth was directed at Imaro!

Knots of rock-hard muscle writhed across the arms and shoulders of the Azuth that was Bomunu. It moved on the granite throne. It opened its sabre-filled mouth and roared; the chilling sound of that cry reverberated through the chamber.

With iron determination, Imaro beat back his rising fear. If this monstrous thing was indeed Bomunu, then at least now he knew what he was fighting. And what he felt for Bomunu was far from fear . . .

As for Tanisha, she stared in horror at these happenings, her incomparable body slick with cold sweat. She swooned.

Imaro leapt into action as the Azuth bounded from its throne and landed with a clatter of hooves upon the stone floor. Bellowing the war cry of the Ilyassai, he moved in to close with his demonic adversary. A hideous grin split the apelike visage of the monstrosity as it leaped toward the barbarian. Surprisingly agile, despite the seven-foot bulk of its misshaped body, its eyes glowed with an intelligence that had never belonged to any beast but man. They were the eyes of Bomunu . . .

Imaro swung his scimitar at the Azuth's belly in a disemboweling thrust. It never reached its target. With incredible speed, the monster lashed out with one hoof and sent Imaro's sword spinning across the floor. A second kick thudded into the warrior's side. A lesser man's ribs would have been caved in at the impact.

The Azuth's third blow was halted in midair by Imaro's cobra-quick hand. Firmly gripping the thin goat-ankle, Imaro kicked its other leg from under it. This caused the Azuth to crash heavily to the stone floor. Imaro leaped astride the fallen monster and brought his malletlike fist down twice, smashing at its gaping mouth. The fist did its work well; the Azuth's formidable fangs broke.

Screeching in pain, the Azuth struck back. One sweep of its immense arm sent Imaro flying through the air, to land in a tumbled heap ten feet away.

Scrambling upright, the combatants faced each other anew, each now having more respect for the other. Imaro knew that he would need his dagger against this formidable opponent; the Azuth was too strong for even him to fight bare-handed. He reached down to draw his dagger— the scabbard was empty! Too late, Imaro recalled that he had given it to Pomphis to use in case the Mizungus caught up with him.

The Azuth, sensing the barbarian's momentary lapse of concentration, clattered across the intervening space and encircled Imaro's body in a deadly bear-hug. Its long, powerful arms began to squeeze with crushing force. Imaro struggled furiously, but was unable to break the iron grip that pinioned his arms to his sides. Harder squeezed the Azuth, all the while glaring at Imaro with the triumphant eyes of Bomunu.

Still did Imaro strive to break free. If only he could free his arms before the beast crushed the breath out of his body . . . he was thankful for the protection of the armor, even though it was made by the accursed Mizungus . . .

Suddenly, the Azuth realized that Imaro was slipping loose. Carrying the big barbarian as though he were weightless, the monster slammed Imaro into the nearest wall. The impact nearly tore Imaro loose from his senses. Pain exploded through his skull. Yet he doggedly fought on, levering his arms upward against the Azuth's body.

Again and again was Imaro pounded viciously against the unyielding granite wall. Only the metal helmet on his head prevented his skull from being split open. Then the helmet fell away.

Blackness crept along the edges of Imaro's consciousness. He knew that he' couldn't take much more punishment. He had to break free. With a supreme effort, dipping deep into the well of his barbarian-bred vitality, his arms slid out of the hold of the Azuth's grip! His fists clubbed against the sides of the beast's bullet head, landing directly on its ears. With a howl of pain, the Azuth fell back. In a reflex action, Imaro shoved out with both feet as he slid to the floor. Dimly, he heard it stumble backwards and fall a dozen feet away. Then he painfully dragged himself to his feet.

Imaro's head was spinning, and his body throbbed in agony and exhaustion. But he still lived, and he could still fight. Already, the Azuth was approaching again, but more slowly this time. Though blood was dripping from its ears and broken mouth, Imaro knew that his own pain was greater than the monster's. But he knew also that the Azuth's seemingly invincible body housed the *n'kaa* of Bomunu. And in Bomunu's eyes he now detected a glimmer of fear . . .

At once a strategem flashed into Imaro's mind.

"Bomunu!" Imaro's deep voice rang out.

The Azuth stopped short at the sound of its true name.

"Bomunu!" he repeated. "Traitor! Coward! Even in the skin of a demon-beast, you cannot hope to best me. You, who sold the lives of five thousand men for a handful of diamonds! Miserable woman-stealer! Were you in the body of Varinga, the swamp dragon, still would I sweep the floor with your useless carcass! Come! Let us see if you dare to match strength again with a *man!*"

Imaro's challenge had its desired effect. Knowing that the Azuth was too powerful to meet in head-on combat,

Imaro had shrewdly goaded the part of it that was Bomunu. Now enraged by Imaro's taunts, the Azuth bellowed like an enraged beast, lowered its head and charged as though it meant to immolate Imaro in one mad rush.

At the last possible moment, however, Imaro ducked under one of the outstretched arms and grabbed its thick wrist. Pivoting on his heel, he let the Azuth's own momentum carry it crashing into the wall.

The Azuth staggered slowly to its impossibly hooved feet. But before it could move, Imaro was upon it like a springing panther. Leaping astride the Azuth's broad back, he locked powerful legs around its sagging middle. Then he cupped his hands under the chin of the monster, and pulled back with all his might. Harder and harder he pulled, seeking to break the creature's neck. At the same time, the Azuth reached back with its long arms and tried to rip him off his body. But the grip of Imaro's legs was vise-like. And Imaro's arms were pulling his head back further and further.

Cords of muscle swelled and rippled across Imaro's back and shoulders as he applied yet more force. Once he had twisted the neck of M'boa the buffalo. The Azuth's neck was no thicker than M'boa's . . .

Now the part of the monster that was Bomunu grew desperate with fear. More pressure was being exerted by the tormentor astride its back; already the neck-bones were beginning to crack audibly. A strangled cry issued from the Azuth's tortured throat. It was the scream of a frightened, dying thing.

One last surge of almost superhuman strength, and the Azuth's neck broke with the sound of a tree snapping. Even as it toppled forward, Imaro could feel the slimy flesh turning back to stone. Having died a second time, the *n'kaa* of Bomunu had now gone to the Death Hell of the Mashataan. Imaro staggered aside as the Azuth crashed to the floor. The god of the Mizungus was now nothing more than a pile of broken rock.

Imaro tried to maintain consciousness and rise to his feet. But the battles he had fought that day, the long miles he had traveled, the tremendous effort of the fight with the Azuth, all these exertions had been enough to sap even Imaro's mighty thews. He sprawled on the floor, breathing in broken pants and gasps.

No time did he have to savor his triumph, his final revenge against Bomunu. Sensing a presence behind him, Imaro painfully managed to turn his aching head. What he saw was the priest of the Mizungus standing over him. On the priest's pale face was an expression of total and insane hatred. And in his hands was Imaro's lost scimitar!

7.   *THE GHOST-HERD*

High over his lank-haired head did the Mizungu lift the sword, to bring it down in a death-stroke for this black interloper who had dared to profane his temple and slay his god. Imaro's reflexes were sluggish with fatigue. Still he attempted to avoid the priest's blow.

Suddenly the Mizungu cried out, more in surprise than pain. His eyes bulged, and Imaro's sword dropped from nerveless fingers. Stiffly, the priest fell forward, dead without knowing it. From his back protruded the hilt of a deep-driven dagger. And behind the corpse stood none other than Pomphis!

For once, the pygmy was not grinning. Apprehension marked his features as he assisted Imaro to his feet. Pomphis spoke hurriedly.

"Haven't you cut that wench free yet, man?" he demanded peevishly. "We've got to get out of here, before that raving mob returns!"

Then, noticing the barbarian's battered condition, Pomphis asked, "What in the name of M'tungi happened to you?"

Too exhausted to speak, Imaro pointed to the empty throne, then to the fragmented remains of the Azuth. Understanding dawned immediately in the Bambuti's eyes. Thanks to his Cushite mentor, Pomphis knew half a dozen ways in which life could be given to inanimate objects.

With slow steps Imaro made his way to the altar that held the bound form of Tanisha. He could feel the strength beginning to flow back into his limbs. The recuperative powers of the warriors of Ilyassai were as legendary as their prowess in war.

Mercifully, the girl's swoon had lasted throughout Imaro's epic battle with the Azuth. Only now were her brown eyes beginning to open. She moaned as Imaro sliced through the leather thongs. Then her eyes opened wide in bafflement. What she saw was a hazy apparition with the battered features of Imaro, atop a body in Mizungu armor, with a huge curved sword in its massive hand.

It came as no wonder, then, that with a small cry, Tanisha promptly fainted again.

Pomphis, who had followed Imaro over to the altar, let out a loud snort of disgust.

"Now we'll have to carry her out of here, curse the luck! Hurry; we haven't got all night."

Imaro was about to retort, when the sounds of the returning Mizungus rolled down the hallway and burst like a wave about them.

"Too late!" cried Pomphis.

Imaro agreed. "But we'll at least take many of them with us before we die."

The first of the Mizungu horde pushed out of the darkness and into view. Many of them had armed themselves with long swords and wicked hooked knives.

Imaro brandished his sword menacingly, daring the Mizungus to come forth and die upon its edge. Pomphis presented a defiant little figure, though inwardly he wished he weren't there.

More of the Mizungus crowded into the chamber. When they saw their priest was dead and their god destroyed, their rage was terrible to behold. As one, they charged furiously across the chamber, clearly intending to tear the blacks into bloody pieces.

Imaro watched the black skulls bobbing against the Mizungus' waists. He remembered that he would have to kill Tanisha before the Mizungus got to her . . . THE SKULLS! At once the barbarian remembered what had happened when the priest had smashed Bomunu's skull . . . and he remembered what he had seen in the carvings on the temple's outside wall . . .

Imaro bounded over to where the priest's body lay. As Pomphis looked on in utter astonishment, the barbarian systematically smashed all of the skulls encircling his waist. Imaro paid no heed to the small explosions that accompanied each shattering. But the Mizungus did. Immediately the tenor of their shouting voices changed from fury to fright as eight flame-eyed, spectral wraiths arose from the remains of their prisons.

Like the *n'kaa* of Bomunu, these wispy entities turned their lambent gaze upon Imaro. But he knew that he had nothing to fear from these. Indeed, these *n'kaas* seemed to be expressing gratitude. For these were the last remnants of the people that the Mizungus had slain long ago when they had first settled here. Somehow, the Atlantean priests had found a way to harness the life-force so that the Mizungus could live for centuries, aging only slowly.

The *n'kaas* of these ancient, unfortunate people craved a vengeance more terrible than any that Imaro could ever conceive.

The ghost-things began to fall upon the terror-stricken Mizungus. As soon as the *n'kaas* were fully absorbed into a Mizungu, each host began a grotesque, frenzied kind of dance which ended in his tearing the skull from his waist and smashing it onto the stone floor, thus releasing more *n'kaas*.

As the *n'kaas* sought out new bodies to inhabit, the Mizungus crashed against each other, attempting to flee in panic. Explosions rang throughout the chamber as more and more skulls were shattered, releasing more and more *n'kaas*. The Mizungus fled from the chamber like a herd of frightened deer. And they had good reason to be afraid. For each Mizungu that had been bereft of its dangling black skull, a pile of gray dust lay putrefying on the floor . . .

Shrieks echoed down the dark hallway as the Mizungus fled their temple.

"It isn't safe to remain here any longer," Pomphis said nervously. "These *n'kaas* don't want to harm *us*, but the release of so many of them has unleashed powerful mystic forces. We'd best not remain hereabouts."

"All right," growled Imaro. He gathered up Tanisha, throwing her body across one strong shoulder.

With Pomphis leading the way, they went out of the temple, up the ruined avenue, through the broken gate-portal, and away from the dying city. Its long-overdue destruction was imminent. Insane screams and thundering crashes of falling blocks of stone accompanied their flight from M'ji ya Wazimu, the City of Madness . . .

It was not until they were far, far away that the barbarian and the Bambuti stopped running.

8.   THE END OF IT

The moon still shone brightly through the treetops as Imaro, Pomphis and Tanisha rested quietly in a forest glade. A fire had been built to discourage the bolder predators. Tanisha had regained consciousness, but had sat staring empty-eyed, silent—until she screamed.

Her sudden, piercing shriek must have startled the nocturnal prowlers as much as it did Pomphis and Imaro.

Imaro's reaction was simple and direct. He reached out and struck Tanisha's face with an open-handed blow. Pomphis suspected that there was more to that slap than the mere quieting of an hysterical woman. However he chose to maintain a discreet silence on the matter.

Tanisha's response to Imaro's blow was instantaneous. It had removed her from the nightmare world of leering idols and pale madmen and deposited her quite firmly into the world of reality . . .

She jumped to her feet and screeched, "Who do you think you're hitting, you big ape? Where are we, anyway. How did you get away from the Kakassa?"

Imaro related the tale of his escape and his tracking of Bomunu into the unknown forest, and the events that followed.

"The nature of your trail," he said darkly, "indicated that you did not resist Bomunu very strongly."

"So *that's* it," thought Pomphis, as he listened in the background.

Placing her hands firmly on her hips, Tanisha retorted, "He said he was going to kill me if I didn't go with him. Besides, I thought you were dead. I saw you fall after decimating half the Azanian army."

"The women of my tribe," Imaro growled, "would kill themselves before allowing themselves to be taken by a man other than their own."

"Do you know any who did?" Tanisha shot back, mockery showing on her piquant ebon face.

Imaro thought for a moment. Then he shook his head.

Tanisha's face softened, and she walked into Imaro's arms, pressing her warm body close to his, burying her kinky-crowned head into his broad chest. Then she looked up at him and said,

"Poor Imaro. Strong enough to knock down an elephant, but with so much to learn about women."

Imaro silenced her with a fierce kiss.

Pomphis cleared his throat and interjected, "I suppose that I shall be standing the first watch."

Pomphis was about to turn away to begin his watch when Imaro asked him a question that had been plaguing him for some time.

"Just what was it you shouted to the Mizungus that drove them mad, back there in the temple?"

Pomphis grinned hugely. "It's all quite simple. You see, the highest Mashataan in the Atlantean pantheon is named M'wa-Thuu. So in their language, I said 'M'wa-Thuu eats giraffe dung!' That was one of our ancestors' favorite battle-cries during the Mizungu War . . ."

For the first time in many days, Imaro threw back his head and laughed long and loudly. The others joined him. The events of this night would haunt their memories for a long time to come. But for now, they could send their laughter rolling up against the bright, sardonic moon.

Jack Vance

THE SEVENTEEN VIRGINS

What can I possibly say about Jack Vance, that hasn't already been said by astute critics even more admiring of his talents than I? His delicious style, his languid prose, his sparkling flow of imaginative invention, and his infinite variety, have all been pointed out many times before. Let me say this, though: it is a sorry year for fantasy, that does not have a new Dying Earth story published sometime during its span. Luckily, 1974 was a good year in this respect; and the Dying Earth story is not only a Dying Earth story, but the first in a whole new cycle of the adventures of that inimitable and charming rogue, that very thief of thieves, Cugel the Clever . . . so enjoy!

—LC

Cugel, having made a hasty departure from Julle, found himself on foot in that dismal tract of rolling bone-colored hills known as the Pale Rugates. As he trudged south, up ridge, down swale, Cugel, never a stolid individual, was affected by a variety of emotions. To his elation, he had baffled his pursuers, but only by plunging recklessly into the wilderness, which was cause for a corresponding anxiety. Baleful creatures such as sindis, shambs, erbs and grues shunned the Pale Rugates, for which Cugel gave heartfelt thanks, but the reason for such avoidance was the stark inhospitability of the region. The breadth of the

145

sky exalted his soul; the emptiness of the far distances caused him fatigue and despondency; and so it went.

For want of better entertainment Cugel gave expression to his emotions, alternating cries of anger for the indignities he had suffered at Julle with laughter for the confusion of his enemies. His immediate discomfort provoked him to curses; the prospect of even harsher conditions clamped at his throat and stifled his voice completely. During the first day or two, in spasms of self-assertion, he would throw his fists over his head and shout to the sky: "Hear me, all who detect sound, in every realm of the living world! I am Cugel, Cugel the Clever! My courage and resource, my cunning and craft are notorious! I am not to be trifled with!"

Such diversion presently lost its edge, and Cugel marched south in silence: up slope, out on the ridge, there to overlook a far succession of barren swells, pallid as parchment and given substance by the intervening shadows; down again into the hollow where at rare intervals a seep of water nourished a sickly vegetation.

Day followed day. The sun rose cool and dim, swam languidly up into the dark-blue sky, from time to time seeming to lurch, or tremble, or flicker with a film of blue-black luster, finally to settle like an enormous purple pearl behind the western horizon. In the marches Cugel found ramp and burdock and newts which provided him sustenance; by night he huddled into the bracken.

On the afternoon of the seventh day Cugel limped down a slope into an ancient orchard, long abandoned. A few withered hag-apples clung to the limbs; these Cugel avidly devoured. Then, discerning the trace of an old road, he set off buoyed by the conviction that the Pale Rugates lay behind him.

The track in due course led out upon a slope overlooking a broad plain. A river swung up to the outlying shoulders of the Pale Rugates, skirted a small town immediately below, then disappeared into the southwest haze.

Cugel surveyed the landscape with keen attention. Out upon the plain he saw carefully tended garden plots, each precisely square and of identical size; along the river drifted a fisherman's punt. A placid scene, thought Cugel. On the other hand, the town was built to a strange and archaic architecture, and the scrupulous precision with which the houses surrounded the square suggested a like inflexibility in the inhabitants. The houses themselves were no less uniform, each a construction of two, or three, or even four squat bulbs of diminishing size, one on the other, the lowest always painted blue, the second dark red, the third and fourth respectively a dull mustard ocher and black; and each house terminated in a spire of fancifully twisted iron rods, of greater or lesser height. An inn on the riverbank showed a style somewhat looser and easier, with a pleasant garden surrounding. Along the river road to the east Cugel now noticed the approach of a caravan of six high-wheeled wagons, and his uncertainty dissolved; the town was evidently tolerant of strangers, and Cugel confidently set off down the hill.

At the outskirts to town he halted and drew forth his purse which hung loose and limp. Cugel examined the contents: five terces, a sum hardly adequate to his needs. Cugel reflected a moment, then collected a handful of pebbles which he dropped into the purse, to create a reassuring rotundity. He dusted his breeches, adjusted his green hunter's cap, and proceeded.

He entered the town without challenge or even attention. Crossing the square, he halted to inspect a contrivance even more peculiar than the quaint architecture: a stone fire pit in which several logs blazed high, rimmed by five lamps on iron stands, each with five wicks, and above an intricate linkage of mirrors and lenses, the purpose of which surpassed Cugel's comprehension. Two young men tended the device with diligence, trimming the twenty-five wicks, prodding the fire, adjusting screws and levers which in turn controlled the mirrors and lenses. They wore what appeared to be the local costume: voluminous blue knee-length breeches, red shirts, brass-buttoned black vests and broad-brimmed hats; after disinterested glances they paid Cugel no heed, and he continued to the inn.

In the adjacent garden two dozen folk of the town sat at tables, eating and drinking with great gusto. Cugel watched them a moment or two; their punctilio and elegant gestures suggested the manners of an age far past. Like their houses, they were a sort unique to Cugel's experience, pale and thin, with egg-shaped heads, long noses, dark expressive eyes and ears cropped in various styles.

The men were uniformly bald and their pates glistened in the red sunlight. The women parted their black hair in the middle, then cut it abruptly short a half-inch above the ears, a style which Cugel considered unbecoming. Watching the folk eat and drink, Cugel was unfavorably reminded of the fare which had sustained him across the Pale Rugates, and he gave no further thought to his five terces. He strode into the garden and seated himself at a table. A portly man in a blue apron approached, frowning somewhat at Cugel's disheveled appearance. Cugel immediately brought forth two terces which he handed to the man. "This is for yourself, my good fellow, to insure expeditious service. I have just completed an arduous journey; I am famished with hunger. You may bring me a platter identical to that which the gentleman yonder is enjoying, together with a selection of side dishes and a bottle of wine. Then be so good as to ask the innkeeper to prepare me a comfortable chamber." Cugel carelessly brought forth his purse and dropped it upon the table where its weight produced an impressive implication. "I will also require a bath, fresh linen and a barber."

"I myself am Maier the innkeeper," said the portly man in a gracious voice. "I will see to your wishes immediately."

"Excellent," said Cugel. "I am impressed with your establishment, and will remain several days."

The innkeeper bowed in gratification and hurried off to supervise the preparation of Cugel's dinner.

Cugel made an excellent meal, though the second course, a dish of crayfish stuffed with mince and slivers of scarlet mangoneel, he found a trifle too rich. The roast fowl however could not be faulted, and the wine pleased Cugel to such an extent that he ordered a second flask. Maier the innkeeper served the bottle himself and accepted Cugel's compliments with a trace of complacency. "There is no better wine in Gundar! It is admittedly expensive, but you are a person who appreciates the best."

"Precisely true," said Cugel. "Sit down and take a glass with me. I confess to curiosity in regard to this remarkable town."

The innkeeper willingly complied. "I am puzzled that

you find Gundar remarkable. I have lived here all my life, and it seems ordinary enough to me."

"I will cite three circumstances which I consider worthy of note," said Cugel, now somewhat expansive by reason of the wine. "First: the bulbous construction of your buildings. Secondly: the contrivance of lenses above the fire, which at the very least must stimulate a stranger's interest. Thirdly: the fact that the men of Gundar are all stark bald."

The innkeeper nodded thoughtfully. "The architecture at least is quickly explained. The ancient Gunds lived in enormous gourds. When a section of the wall became weak, it was replaced with a board, until in due course the folk found themselves living in houses fashioned completely of wood, and the style has persisted. As for the fire and the projectors, do you not know the world-wide Order of Solar Emosynaries? We stimulate the vitality of the sun; so long as our beam of sympathetic vibration regulates solar combustion, it will never expire. Similar stations exist at other locations: at Blue Azor; on the Isle of Brazel; at the walled city Munt; and in the observatory of the Grand Starkeeper at Vir Vassilis."

Cugel shook his head sadly. "I fear that conditions have changed. Brazel has long since sunk beneath the waves. Munt was destroyed a thousand years ago by Dystropes. I have never heard of either Blue Azor or Vir Vassilis, though I am widely traveled. Possibly, here at Gundar, you are the solitary Solar Emosynaries yet in existence."

"This is dismal news," declared Maier. "The noticeable enfeeblement of the sun is hereby explained. Perhaps we had best double the fire under our regulator."

Cugel poured more wine. "A question leaps to mind. If, as I suspect, this is the single Solar Emosynary station yet in operation, who or what regulates the sun when it has passed below the horizon?"

The innkeeper shook his head. "I can offer no explanation. It may be that during the hours of night the sun itself relaxes and, as it were, sleeps, although this is of course sheerest speculation."

"Allow me to offer another hypothesis," said Cugel. "Conceivably the waning of the sun has advanced beyond all possibility of regulation, so that your efforts, though formerly useful, are now ineffective."

Maier threw up his hands in perplexity. "These complications surpass my scope, but yonder stands the Nolde Huruska." He directed Cugel's attention to a large man with a deep chest, a heavy muscular belly, and a bristling black beard, who stood at the entrance. "Excuse me a moment." He rose to his feet and approaching the Nolde spoke for several minutes, indicating Cugel from time to marched across the garden to confront Cugel. He spoke in time. The Nolde finally made a brusque gesture and a heavy voice: "I understand you to assert that no Emosynaries exist other than ourselves?"

"I stated nothing so definitely," said Cugel, somewhat on the defensive. "I remarked that I had traveled widely and that no other such 'Emosynary' agency has come to my attention; and I innocently speculated that possibly none now operate."

"At Gundar we conceive of 'innocence' as a positive quality, not merely an insipid absence of guilt," stated the Nolde. "We are not the fools that certain untidy ruffians might suppose."

Cugel suppressed the hot remark which rose to his lips and contented himself with a shrug. Maier walked away with the Nolde, and for several minutes the two men conferred, with frequent glances in Cugel's direction. Then the Nolde departed and the innkeeper returned to Cugel's table. "A somewhat brusque man, the Nolde of Gundar," he told Cugel, "but competent withal."

"It would be presumptuous for me to comment," said Cugel. "What, precisely, is his function?"

"At Gundar we place great store upon precision and methodicity," explained Maier. "We feel that the absence of order encourages disorder, and the official responsible for the inhibition of caprice and abnormality is the Nolde . . . What was our previous conversation? Ah, yes, you mentioned our notorious baldness. I can offer no definite explanation. According to our savants, the condition signifies the final perfection of the human race. Other folk give credence to an ancient legend. A pair of magicians, Astherlin and Mauldred, vied for the favor of the Gunds. Astherlin promised the boon of extreme hairiness, so that the folk of Gundar need never wear garments. Mauldred, to the contrary, offered the Gunds baldness, with all the consequent advantages, and easily won the contest; in fact Mauldred became the first Nolde of Gundar, the post now filled, as you know, by Huruska." Maier the innkeeper pursed his lips and looked off across the garden. "Huruska, a distrustful sort, has reminded me of my fixed rule to ask all transient guests to settle their accounts on a daily basis. I naturally assured him of your complete reliability, but simply in order to appease Huruska, I will tender the reckoning in the morning."

"This is tantamount to an insult," declared Cugel haughtily. "Must we truckle to the whims of Huruska? Not I, you may be assured! I will settle my account in the usual manner."

The innkeeper blinked. "May I ask how long you intend to stay?"

"My journey takes me south, by the most expeditious transport available, which I assume to be riverboat."

"The town Lumarth lies ten days by caravan across the Lirrh Aing. The Isk River also flows past Lumarth, but is judged inconvenient by virtue of three intervening localities. The Lallo Marsh is infested with stinging insects; the tree dwarfs of the Santalba Forest pelt passing boats with refuse; and the Desperate Rapids shatter both bones and boats."

"In this case I will travel by caravan," said Cugel. "Meanwhile I will remain here, unless the persecutions of Huruska become intolerable."

Maier licked his lips and looked over his shoulder. "I assured Huruska that I would adhere to the strict letter of my rule. He will surely make a great issue of the matter unless—"

Cugel made a gracious gesture. "Bring me seals. I will close up my purse, which contains a fortune in opals and alumes. We will deposit the purse in your strongbox, and you may hold it for surety. Even Huruska cannot now protest!"

Maier held up his hands in awe. "I could not undertake so large a responsibility!"

"Dismiss all fear," said Cugel. "I have protected the purse with a spell; the instant a criminal breaks the seal the jewels are transformed into pebbles."

Maier dubiously accepted Cugel's purse on these terms. They jointly saw the seals applied and the purse put into Maier's strongbox.

Cugel now repaired to his chamber, where he bathed, commanded the services of a barber and dressed in fresh garments. Setting his cap at an appropriate angle, he strolled out upon the square.

His steps led him to the Solar Emosynary station. As before, two young men worked diligently, one stoking the blaze and adjusting the five lamps, while the other held the regulatory beam fixed upon the low sun.

Cugel inspected the contrivance from all angles, and presently the person who fed the blaze called out: "Are you not that notable traveler who today expressed doubts as to the efficacy of the Emosynary system?"

Cugel spoke carefully: "I told Maier and Huruska this: that Brazel is sunk below the Melantine Gulf and almost gone from memory; that the walled city Munt was long ago laid waste; that I am acquainted with neither Blue Azor, nor Vir Vassilis. These were my only positive statements."

The young fire stoker petulantly threw an armload of logs into the fire pit. "Still we are told that you consider our efforts impractical."

"I would not care to go so far," said Cugel politely. "Even if the other Emosynary agencies are abandoned, it is possible that the Gundar regulator suffices. Who knows?"

"I will tell you this," declared the stoker. "We work without recompense, and in our spare time we must cut and transport fuel. The process is tedious."

The operator of the aiming device amplified his friend's complaint. "Huruska and the elders do none of the work; they merely ordain that we toil, which of course is the easiest part of the project. Janred and I are of a sophisticated new generation; on principle we reject all dogmatic doctrines. I, for one, consider the Solar Emosynary system a waste of time and effort."

"If the other agencies are abandoned," argued Janred the stoker, "who or what regulates the sun when it has passed beyond the horizon? The system is pure balderdash."

The operator of the lenses declared: "I will now demonstrate as much and free us all from this thankless toil!" He worked a lever. "Notice! I direct the regulatory beam away from the sun. Look! It shines as before, without the slightest attention on our part!"

Cugel inspected the sun, and for a fact it seemed to glow as before, flickering from time to time, and shivering like an old man with the ague. The two young men watched with similar interest, and as minutes passed, they began to murmur in satisfaction. "We are vindicated! The sun has not gone out!"

Even as they watched, the sun, perhaps fortuitously, underwent a cachectic spasm, and lurched alarmingly toward the horizon. Behind them sounded a bellow of outrage, and the Nolde Huruska ran forward. "What is the meaning of this irresponsibility? Direct the regulator aright and instantly! Would you have us groping the rest of our lives in the dark?"

The stoker resentfully jerked his thumb toward Cugel. "He convinced us that the system was unnecessary and that our work was futile."

"What!" Huruska swung his formidable body about and confronted Cugel. "Only hours ago you set foot in Gundar, and already you are disrupting the fabric of our existence! I warn you, our patience is not illimitable! Be off with you and do not approach the Emosynary agency a second time!"

Choking with fury, Cugel swung on his heel and marched off across the square.

At the caravan terminal he inquired as to transport southward, but the caravan which had arrived at noon would on the morrow depart eastward the way it had come.

Cugel returned to the inn and stepped into the tavern. He noticed three men playing a card game and posted himself as an observer. The game proved to be a simple version of Zampolio, and presently Cugel asked if he might join the play. "But only if the stakes are not too high," he protested. "I am not particularly skillful, and I dislike losing more than a terce or two."

"Bah," exclaimed one of the players. "What is money? Who will spend it when we are dead?"

"If we take all your gold, then you need not carry it further," another remarked jocularly.

"All of us must learn," the third player assured Cugel. "You are fortunate to have the three premier experts of Gundar as instructors."

Cugel drew back in alarm. "I refuse to lose more than a single terce!"

"Come now! Don't be a prig!"

"Very well," said Cugel. "I will risk it. But these cards are tattered and dirty. By chance I have a fresh set in my pouch."

"Excellent! The game proceeds!"

Two hours later the three Gunds threw down their cards, gave Cugel long hard looks, then as if with a single mind rose to their feet and departed the tavern. Inspecting his gains, Cugel counted thirty-two terces and a few odd coppers. In a cheerful frame of mind he retired to his chamber for the night.

In the morning as he consumed his breakfast, he noticed the arrival of the Nolde Huruska, who immediately engaged Maier the innkeeper in conversation. A few minutes later Huruska approached Cugel's table and stared down at Cugel with a somewhat menacing grin, while Maier stood anxiously a few paces to the rear.

Cugel spoke in a voice of strained politeness: "Well, what is it this time? The sun has risen; my innocence in the matter of the regulatory beam has been established."

"I am concerned with another matter. Are you acquainted with our penalties for fraud?"

Cugel shrugged. "The matter is of no interest to me."

"They are severe and I will revert to them in a moment. First, let me inquire: Did you entrust to Maier a purse purportedly containing valuable jewels?"

"I did indeed. The property is protected by a spell, I may add; if the seal is broken, the gems become ordinary pebbles."

Huruska exhibited the purse. "Notice, the seal is intact. I cut a slit in the leather and looked within. The contents were then and are now—" with a flourish Huruska turned the purse out upon the table "—pebbles identical to those in the road yonder."

Cugel exclaimed in outrage, "The jewels are now worthless rubble! I hold you responsible and you must make recompense!"

Huruska uttered an offensive laugh. "If you can change gems to pebbles, you can change pebbles to gems. Maier will now tender the bill. If you refuse to pay, I intend to have you nailed into the enclosure under the gallows until such a time as you change your mind."

"Your insinuations are both disgusting and absurd," declared Cugel. "Innkeeper, present your account! Let us finish with this farrago once and for all."

Maier came forward with a slip of paper. "I make the total to be eleven terces, plus whatever gratuities might seem in order."

"There will be no gratuities," said Cugel. "Do you harass all your guests in this fashion?" He flung eleven terces down. "Take your money and leave me in peace."

Maier sheepishly gathered up the coins; Huruska made an inarticulate sound and turned away. Cugel, upon finishing his breakfast, went out once more to stroll across the square. Here he met an individual whom he recognized to be the potboy in the tavern, and Cugel signaled him to a halt. "You seem an alert and knowledgeable fellow," said Cugel. "May I inquire your name?"

"I am generally known as 'Zeller.' "

"I would guess you to be well acquainted with the folk of Gundar."

"I consider myself well-informed. Why do you ask?"

"First," said Cugel, "let me ask if you care to turn your knowledge to profit?"

"Certainly, so long as I evade the attention of the Nolde."

"Very good. I notice a disused booth yonder which should serve our purpose. In one hour we shall put our enterprise into operation."

Cugel returned to the inn, where at his request Maier brought a board, a brush and paint. Cugel composed a sign:

THE EMINENT SEER CUGEL
COUNSELS, INTERPRETS,
PROGNOSTICATES.
ASK YOU WILL BE ANSWERED!
CONSULTATIONS:
THREE TERCES.

Cugel hung the sign above the booth, arranged curtains and waited for customers. The potboy, meanwhile, had inconspicuously secreted himself at the back.

Almost immediately folk crossing the square halted to read the sign. A woman of early middle-age presently came forward. "Three terces is a large sum. What results can you guarantee?"

"None whatever, by the very nature of things. I am a skilled voyant, I have acquaintance with the arts of magic, but knowledge comes to me from unknown and uncontrollable sources."

The woman paid over her money. "Three terces is cheap if you can resolve my worries. My daughter all her life has enjoyed the best of health, but now she ails and suffers a morose condition. All my remedies are to no avail. What must I do?"

"A moment, madame, while I meditate." Cugel drew the curtain and leaned back to where he could hear the potboy's whispered remarks, then once again drew aside the curtains.

"I have made myself one with the cosmos! Knowledge has entered my mind! Your daughter Dilian is pregnant. For an additional three terces I will supply the father's name."

"This is a fee I pay with pleasure," declared the woman grimly. She paid, received the information and marched purposefully away.

Another woman approached, paid three terces, and Cugel addressed himself to her problem. "My husband assured me that he had put by a canister of gold coins against the future, but upon his death I could find not so much as a copper. Where has he hidden it?"

Cugel closed the curtains, took counsel with the potboy and again appeared to the woman. "I have discouraging news for you. Your husband Finister spent much of his hoarded gold at the tavern. With the rest he purchased an amethyst brooch for a woman named Varletta."

The news of Cugel's remarkable abilities spread rapidly, and trade was brisk. Shortly before noon, a large woman, muffled and veiled, approached the booth, paid three terces, and asked in a high-pitched, if husky, voice: "Read me my fortune!"

Cugel drew the curtain and consulted the potboy, who was at a loss. "It is no one I know. I can tell you nothing."

"No matter," said Cugel. "My suspicions are verified." He drew aside the curtain. "The portents are unclear and I refuse to take your money." Cugel returned the fee. "I can tell you this much: you are an individual of domineering character and no great intelligence. Ahead lies what? Honors? A long voyage by water? Revenge on your enemies? Wealth? The image is distorted; I may be reading my own future."

The woman tore away her veils and stood revealed as the Nolde Huruska. "Master Cugel, you are lucky indeed that you returned my money; otherwise I would have taken you up for deceptive practices. In any event, I deem your activities mischievous and contrary to the public interest. Gundar is in an uproar because of your revelations; there will be no more of them. Take down your sign and be happily thankful that you have escaped so easily."

"I will be glad to terminate my enterprise," said Cugel with dignity. "The work is taxing."

Huruska stalked away in a huff. Cugel divided his earnings with the potboy, and in a spirit of mutual satisfaction they departed the booth.

Cugel dined on the best that the inn afforded, but later when he went into the tavern, he discovered a noticeable lack of amiability among the patrons and presently went off to his chamber.

The next morning as he took breakfast, a caravan of ten wagons arrived in town. The principal cargo appeared to be a bevy of seventeen beautiful maidens, who rode upon two of the wagons. Three other wagons served as dormitories, while the remaining five were loaded with stores, trunks, bales and cases. The caravan master, a portly mild-seeming man with flowing brown hair and a silky beard, assisted his delightful charges to the ground and led them all to the inn, where Maier served up an ample breakfast of spiced porridge, preserved quince, and tea.

Cugel watched the group as they made their meal and reflected that a journey to almost any destination in such company would be a pleasant journey indeed.

The Nolde Huruska appeared and went to pay his respects to the caravan leader. The two conversed amiably at some length, while Cugel waited impatiently.

Huruska at last departed. The maidens, having finished their meal, went off to stroll about the square. Cugel crossed to the table where the caravan leader sat. "Sir, my name is Cugel, and I would appreciate a few words with you."

"By all means! Please be seated. Will you take a glass of excellent tea?"

"Thank you. First, may I inquire the destination of your caravan?"

The caravan leader showed surprise at Cugel's ignorance. "We are bound for Lumarth; these are the 'Seventeen Virgins of Symnathis' who traditionally grace the Grand Pageant."

"I am a stranger to this region," Cugel explained. "Hence I know nothing of the local customs. In any event, I myself am bound for Lumarth and would be pleased to travel with your caravan."

The caravan leader gave an affable assent. "I would be delighted to have you with us."

"Excellent!" said Cugel. "Then all is arranged."

The caravan leader stroked his silky brown beard. "I must warn you that my fees are somewhat higher than usual, owing to the expensive amenities I am obliged to provide these seventeen maidens."

"Indeed," said Cugel. "How much do you require?"

"The journey occupies the better part of ten days, and my minimum charge is twenty terces per diem, for a total of two hundred terces, plus a twenty-terce supplement for wine."

"This is far more than I can afford," said Cugel in a bleak voice. "At the moment I command only a third of this sum. Is there some means by which I might earn my passage?"

"Unfortunately not," said the caravan leader. "Only this morning the position of armed guard was open, which even paid a small stipend, but Huruska the Nolde, who wishes to visit Lumarth, has agreed to serve in this capacity, and the post is now filled."

Cugel made a sound of disappointment and raised his eyes to the sky. When at last he could bring himself to speak, he asked, "When do you plan to depart?"

"Tomorrow at dawn, with absolute punctuality. I am sorry that we will not have the pleasure of your company."

"I share your sorrow," said Cugel. He returned to his own table and sat brooding. Presently he went into the tavern, where various card games were in progress. Cugel attempted to join the play, but in every case his request was denied. In a surly mood he went to the counter where Maier the innkeeper unpacked a crate of earthenware goblets. Cugel tried to initiate a conversation, but for once Maier could take no time from his labors. "The Nolde Huruska goes off on a journey, and tonight his friends mark the occasion with a farewell party, for which I must make careful preparations."

Cugel took a mug of beer to a side table and gave himself to reflection. After a few moments he went out the back exit and surveyed the prospect, which here overlooked the Isk River. Cugel sauntered down to the water's edge and discovered a dock at which the fishermen moored their punts and dried their nets. Cugel looked up and down the river, then returned up the path to the inn to spend the rest of the day watching the seventeen maidens as they strolled about the square or sipped sweet lime tea in the garden of the inn.

The sun set; twilight the color of old wine darkened into night. Cugel set about his preparations, which were quickly achieved, inasmuch as the essence of his plan lay in its simplicity.

The caravan leader, whose name, so Cugel learned, was Shimilko, assembled his exquisite company for their evening meal, then herded them carefully to the dormitory wagons, despite the pouts and protests of those who wished to remain at the inn to enjoy the festivities of the evening.

In the tavern the farewell party in honor of Huruska had already commenced. Cugel seated himself in a dark corner and presently attracted the attention of the perspiring Maier. Cugel produced ten terces. "I admit that I have harbored ungrateful thoughts toward Huruska," he said. "Now I wish to express my good wishes—in absolute anonymity, however! Whenever Huruska starts upon a mug of ale, I want you to place another full mug before him, so that his evening will be incressantly merry. If he asks who has bought the drink, you are only to reply: 'One of your friends wishes to pay you a compliment.' Is this clear?"

"Absolutely, and I will do as you command. It is a large-hearted gesture, which Huruska will appreciate."

The evening progressed. Huruska's friends sang jovial songs and proposed a dozen toasts, in all of which Huruska joined. As Cugel had required, whenever Huruska so much as started to drink from a mug, another was placed at his elbow, and Cugel marveled at Huruska's internal reservoirs.

At last Huruska was prompted to excuse himself from the company. He staggered out the back exit and made his way to that stone wall with a trough below, which had been placed for the convenience .of the tavern's patrons.

As Huruska faced the wall, Cugel stepped behind him and flung a fisherman's net over Huruska's head, then expertly dropped a noose around Huruska's burly shoulders, followed by other turns and ties. Huruska's bellows were drowned by the song at this moment being sung in his honor.

Cugel dragged the cursing hulk down the path to the dock and rolled him over and into a punt. Untying the mooring line, Cugel pushed the punt out into the current of the river. "At the very least," Cugel told himself, "two parts of my prophecy are accurate; Huruska has been honored in the tavern and now is about to enjoy a voyage by water."

He returned to the tavern where Huruska's absence had at last been noticed. Maier expressed the opinion that, with an early departure in the offing, Huruska had prudently retired to bed, and all conceded that this was no doubt the case.

The next morning Cugel arose an hour before dawn. He took a quick breakfast, paid Maier his score, then went to where Shimilko ordered his caravan.

"I bring news from Huruska," said Cugel. "Owing to an unfortunate set of personal circumstances, he finds himself unable to make the journey and has commended me to that post for which you had engaged him."

Shimilko shook his head in wonder. "A pity! Yesterday he seemed so enthusiastic! Well, we all must be flexible, and since Huruska cannot join us, I am pleased to accept you in his stead. As soon as we start, I will instruct you in your duties, which are straightforward. You must stand guard by night and take your rest by day, although in the

case of danger I naturally expect you to join in the defense
of the caravan."

"These duties are well within my competence," said Cugel. "I am ready to depart at your convenience."

"Yonder rises the sun," declared Shimilko. "Let us be
off and away for Lumarth."

Ten days later Shimilko's caravan passed through the
Methune Gap, and the great Vale of Coram opened before
them. The brimming Isk wound back and forth, reflecting
a sultry sheen; in the distance loomed the long dark mass
of the Draven Forest. Closer at hand, five domes of shim-
mering gloss marked the site of Lumarth.

Shimilko addressed himself to the company. "Below lies
what remains of the old city Lumarth. Do not be de-
ceived by the domes; they indicate temples at one time
sacred to the five demons Yaunt, Jastenave, Phampoun,
Adelmar and Suul, and hence were preserved during the
Sampathissic Wars.

"The folk of Lumarth are unlike any of your experience. Many are small sorcerers, though Chaladet the
Grand Thururge has proscribed magic within the city pre-
cincts. You may conceive these people to be languid and
wan and dazed by excess sensation, and you will be cor-
rect. All are obsessively rigid in regard to ritual, and all
subscribe to a Doctrine of Absolute Altruism, which com-
pels them to virtue and benevolence. For this reason they
are known as the 'Kind Folk.' A final word in regard to
our journey, which luckily has gone without untoward in-
cident. The wagoneers have driven with skill; Cugel has
vigilantly guarded us by night, and I am well pleased. So
then: onward to Lumarth, and let meticulous discretion
be the slogan!"

The caravan traversed a narrow track down into the
valley, then proceeded along an avenue of rutted stone
under an arch of enormous black mimosa trees.

At a moldering portal opening upon the plaza the caravan was met by five tall men in gowns of embroidered
silks, the splendid double-crowned headgear of the Cora-
mese Thurists lending them an impressive dignity. The five
men were much alike, with pale transparent skins, thin
high-bridged noses, slender limbs and pensive gray eyes.
One who wore a gorgeous gown of mustard-yellow, crim-

son and black raised two fingers in a calm salute. "My friend Shimilko, you have arrived securely with all your blessed cargo. We are well-served and well-pleased."

"The Lirrh Aing was so placid as almost to be dull," said Shimilko. "To be sure, I was fortunate in securing the services of Cugel, who guarded us so well by night that never were our slumbers interrupted."

"Excellent! Well done, Cugel! We will at this time take custody of the precious maidens. Tomorrow you may render your account to the bursar. The Wayfarer's Inn lies yonder, and I counsel you to its comforts."

"Just so! We will all be the better for a few days rest!"

However, Cugel chose not to so indulge himself. At the door to the inn he told Shimilko: "Here we part company, for I must continue along the way. Affairs press on me, and Almery lies far to the west."

"But your stipend, Cugel! You must wait at least until tomorrow, when I can collect certain monies from the bursar. Until then, I am without funds."

Cugel hesitated, but at last was prevailed upon to stay.

An hour later a messenger strode into the inn. "Master Shimilko, you and your company are required to appear instantly before the Grand Thurge on a matter of the utmost importance."

Shimilko looked up in alarm. "Whatever is the matter?"

"I am obliged to tell you nothing more."

With a long face Shimilko led his company across the plaza to the loggia before the old palace, where Chaladet sat on a massive chair. To either side stood the College of Thurists, and all regarded Shimilko with somber expressions.

"What is the meaning of this summons?" inquired Shimilko. "Why do you regard me with such gravity?"

The Thururge spoke in a deep voice: "Shimilko, the seventeen maidens conveyed by you from Symnathis to Lumarth have been examined, and I regret to say that of the seventeen, only two can be classified as virgins. The remaining fifteen have been sexually deflorated."

Shimilko could hardly speak for consternation. "Impossible!" he sputtered. "At Symnathis I undertook the most elaborate precautions. I can display three separate documents certifying the purity of each. There is no room for doubt! You are in error!"

"We are not in error, Master Shimilko. Conditions are as we describe and may easily be verified."

" 'Impossible' and 'incredible' are the only two words which come to mind," cried Shimilko. "Have you questioned the girls themselves?"

"Of course. They merely raise their eyes to the ceiling and whistle between their teeth. Shimilko, how do you explain this heinous outrage?"

"I am perplexed to the point of confusion! The girls embarked upon the journey as pure as the day they were born. This is fact! During each waking instant they never left my area of perception. This is also fact."

"And when you slept?"

"The implausibility is no less extreme. The teamsters invariably retired together in a group. I shared my wagon with the chief teamster, and each of us will vouch for the other. Cugel meanwhile kept watch over the entire camp."

"Alone?"

"A single guard suffices, even though the nocturnal hours are slow and dismal. Cugel, however, never complained."

"Cugel is evidently the culprit!"

Shimilko smilingly shook his head. "Cugel's duties left him no time for illicit activity."

"What if Cugel scamped his duties?"

Shimilko responded patiently, "Remember, each girl rested secure in her private cubicle with a door between herself and Cugel."

"Well, then—what if Cugel opened this door and quietly entered the cubicle?"

Shimilko considered it for a dubious moment and pulled at his silky beard. "In such a case, I suppose the matter might be possible."

The Grand Thururge turned his gaze upon Cugel. "I insist that you make an exact statement upon this sorry affair."

Cugel cried out indignantly, "The investigation is a travesty! My honor has been assailed!"

Chaladet fixed Cugel with a benign, if somewhat chilly, stare. "You will be allowed redemption. Thurists, I place this person in your custody. See to it that he has every opportunity to regain his dignity and self-esteem!"

Cugel roared out a protest which the Grand Thururge

ignored. From his great dais he looked thoughtfully off across the square. "Is it the third or the fourth month?"

"The chronolog has only just left the month of Yaunt to enter the time of Phampoun."

"So be it. By diligence, this licentious rogue may yet earn our love and respect."

A pair of Thurists grasped Cugel's arms and led him across the square. Cugel jerked this way and that to no avail. "Where are you taking me? What is the meaning of this nonsense?"

One of the Thurists replied in a kindly voice, "We are taking you to the Temple of Phampoun, and it is far from nonsense."

"I do not care for any of this," said Cugel. "Take your hands off of me; I intend to leave Lumarth at once."

"You shall be so assisted."

The group marched up worn marble steps, through an enormous arched portal, into an echoing hall, distinguished only by the high dome and an adytum or altar at the far end. Cugel was led into a side chamber, illuminated by high circular windows and paneled with dark-blue wood. An old man in a white gown entered the room and asked, "What have we here? A person suffering affliction?"

"Yes, Cugel has committed a series of abominable crimes, of which he wishes to purge himself."

"A total misstatement!" cried Cugel. "No proof has been adduced, and I was inveigled against my better judgement."

The Thurists, paying no heed, departed, and Cugel was left with the old man, who hobbled to a bench and seated himself. Cugel started to speak, but the old man held up his hand. "Calm yourself! You must remember that we are a benevolent people, lacking all spite or malice. We exist only to help other sentient beings! If a person commits a crime, we are racked with sorrow for the criminal, whom we believe to be the true victim, and we work without compromise that he may renew himself."

"An enlightened viewpoint!" declared Cugel. "Already I feel regeneration!"

"Excellent! Your remarks validate our philosophy; certainly you have negotiated what I will refer to as Phase One of the program."

Cugel frowned. "There are other phases? Are they really necessary?"

"Yes, indeed; these are Phases Two and Three. I should explain that Lumarth has not always adhered to such a policy. During the high years of the Great Magics the city fell under the sway of Yasbane the Obviator, who breached openings into five demon realms and constructed the five temples of Lumarth. You stand now in the Temple of Phampoun."

"Odd," said Cugel, "that a folk so benevolent are such fervent demonists."

"Nothing could be farther from the truth. The Kind Folk of Lumarth expelled Yasbane, to establish the Era of Love, which must now persist until the final waning of the sun. Our love extends to all, even Yasbane's five demons, whom we hope to rescue from their malevolent evil. You will be the latest in a long line of noble individuals who have worked to this end, and such is Phase Two."

Cugel stood limp in consternation. "Such work far exceeds my competence!"

"Everyone feels the same sensation," said the old man. "Nevertheless, Phampoun must be instructed in kindness, consideration and decency; by making this effort, you will know a surge of happy redemption."

"And Phase Three?" croaked Cugel. "What of that?"

"When you achieve your mission, then you shall be gloriously accepted into our brotherhood!" The old man ignored Cugel's groan of dismay. "Let me see now: the month of Yaunt is just now ending, and we enter the month of Phampoun, who is perhaps the most irascible of the five by reason of his sensitive eyes. He becomes enraged by so much as a single glimmer, and you must attempt your persuasions in absolute darkness. Do you have any further questions?"

"Yes, indeed! Suppose Phampoun refuses to mend his ways?"

"This is 'negativistic thinking' which we Kind Folk refuse to recognize. Ignore everything you may have heard in regard to Phampoun's macabre habits! Go forth in confidence!"

Cugel cried out in anguish, "How will I return to enjoy my honors and rewards?"

"No doubt Phampoun, when contrite, will send you

aloft by a means at his disposal," said the old man. "Now I bid you farewell."

"One moment! Where is food and drink? How will I survive?"

"Again we will leave these matters to the discretion of Phampoun." The old man touched a button; the floor opened under Cugel's feet; he slid down a spiral chute at dizzying velocity. The air gradually became syrupy; Cugel struck a film of invisible constriction which burst with a sound like a cork leaving a bottle, and Cugel emerged into a chamber of medium size, illuminated by the glow of a single lamp.

Cugel stood stiff and rigid, hardly daring to breathe. On a dais across the chamber Phampoun sat sleeping in a massive chair, two black hemispheres shuttering his enormous eyes against the light. The gray torso wallowed almost the length of the dais; the massive splayed legs were planted flat to the floor. Arms, as large around as Cugel himself, terminated in fingers three feet long, each bedecked with a hundred jeweled rings. Phampoun's head was as large as a wheelbarrow, with a huge snout and an enormous loose-wattled mouth. The two eyes, each the size of a dishpan, could not be seen for the protective hemispheres.

Cugel, holding his breath in fear and also against the stench which hung in the air, looked cautiously about the room. A cord ran from the lamp, across the ceiling, to dangle beside Phampoun's fingers; almost as a reflex Cugel detached the cord from the lamp. He saw a single egress from the chamber: a low iron door directly behind Phampoun's chair. The chute by which he had entered was now invisible.

The flaps beside Phampoun's mouth twitched and lifted; a homunculus growing from the end of Phampoun's tongue peered forth. It stared at Cugel with beady black eyes. "Ha, has time gone by so swiftly?" The creature, leaning forward, consulted a mark on the wall. "It has indeed; I have overslept and Phampoun will be cross. What is your name and what are your crimes? These details are of interest to Phampoun—which is to say myself, though from whimsy I usually call myself Pulsifer, as if I were a separate entity."

Cugel spoke in a voice of brave conviction: "I am Cugel, inspector for the new regime which now holds sway in Lumarth. I descended to verify Phampoun's comfort, and since all is well, I will now return aloft. Where is the exit?"

Pulsifer asked plaintively, "You have no crimes to relate? This is harsh news. Both Phampoun and I enjoy great evils. Not long ago a certain sea trader, whose name evades me, held us enthralled for over an hour."

"And then what occurred?"

"Best not to ask." Pulsifer busied himself polishing one of Phampoun's tusks with a small brush. He thrust his head forth and inspected the mottled visage above him. "Phampoun still sleeps soundly; he ingested a prodigious meal before retiring. Excuse me while I check the progress of Phampoun's digestion." Pulsifer ducked back behind Phampoun's wattles and revealed himself only by a vibration in the corded gray neck. Presently he returned to view. "He is quite famished, or so it would appear. I had best wake him; he will wish to converse with you before . . ."

"Before what?"

"No matter."

"A moment," said Cugel. "I am interested in conversing with you rather than Phampoun."

"Indeed?" asked Pulsifer, and polished Phampoun's fang with great vigor. "This is pleasant to hear; I receive few compliments."

"Strange! I see much in you to commend. Necessarily your career goes hand in hand with that of Phampoun, but perhaps you have goals and ambitions of your own?"

Pulsifer propped up Phampoun's lip with his cleaning brush and relaxed upon the ledge so created. "Sometimes I feel that I would enjoy seeing something of the outer world. We have ascended several times to the surface, but always by night when heavy clouds obscure the stars, and even then Phampoun complains of the excessive glare, and he quickly returns below."

"A pity," said Cugel. "By day there is much to see. The scenery surrounding Lumarth is pleasant. The Kind Folk are about to present their Grand Pageant of Ultimate Contrasts, which is said to be most picturesque."

Pulsifer gave his head a wistful shake. "I doubt if ever I will see such events. Have you witnessed many horrid crimes?"

"Indeed I have. For instance, I recall a dwarf of the Batvar Forest who rode a pelgrane—"

Pulsifer interrupted him with a gesture. "A moment. Phampoun will want to hear this." He leaned precariously from the cavernous mouth to peer up toward the shuttered eyeballs. "Is he, or more accurately, am I awake? I thought I noted a twitch. In any event, though I have enjoyed our conversation, we must get on with our duties. Hm, the light cord is disarranged. Perhaps you will be good enough to extinguish the light."

"There is no hurry," said Cugel. "Phampoun sleeps peacefully; let him enjoy his rest. I have something to show you, a game of skill and chance. Are you acquainted with 'Zampolio'?"

Pulsifer signified in the negative, and Cugel produced his cards. "Notice carefully! I deal you four cards and I take four cards, which we conceal from each other." Cugel explained the rules of the game. "Necessarily we play for coins or gold or some such commodity, to make the game interesting. I therefore wager five terces, which you must match."

"Yonder in two sacks is Phampoun's gold, or with equal propriety, my gold, since I am an integral adjunct to this vast hulk. Take forth gold sufficient to equal your terces."

The game proceeded. Pulsifer won the first sally, to his delight, then lost the next, which prompted him to fill the air with dismal complaints; then he won again and again until Cugel declared himself lacking further funds. "You are a clever player indeed; it is a joy to match wits with you! Still, I feel I could beat you had I the sack of terces I left above in the temple."

Pulsifer, somewhat puffed and vainglorious, scoffed at Cugel's boast. "I fear that I am too clever for you! Here, take back your terces and we will play the game once again."

"No, this is not the way sportsmen behave; I am too proud to accept your money. Let me suggest a solution to the problem. In the temple above is my sack of terces and a parcel of sweetmeats which you might wish to consume as we continue our game. Let us go fetch these articles; then I defy you to win as before!"

Pulsifer leaned far out to inspect Phampoun's visage.

"He appears quite comfortable, though his organs are roiling with hunger."

"He sleeps as soundly as ever," declared Cugel. "Let us hurry. If he wakes, our game will be spoiled."

Pulsifer hesitated. "What of Phampoun's gold? We dare not leave it unguarded!"

"We will take it with us, and it will never be outside the range of our vigilance."

"Very well, place it here on the dais."

"So, and now I am ready. How do we go aloft?"

"Merely press the leaden bulb beside the arm of the chair, but please make no untoward disturbance. Phampoun might well be exasperated should he awake in unfamiliar surroundings."

"He has never rested easier! We go aloft!" He pressed the button; the dais shivered and creaked and floated up a dark shaft which opened above them. Presently they burst through the valve of constrictive essence which Cugel had penetrated on his way down the chute. At once a glimmer of scarlet light seeped into the shaft, and a moment later the dais glided to a halt level with the altar in the Temple of Phampoun.

"Now then, my sack of terces," said Cugel. "Exactly where did I leave it? Just over yonder, I believe. Notice! Through the great arches you may overlook the main plaza of Lumarth, and those are the Kind Folk going about their ordinary affairs. What is your opinion of all this?"

"Most interesting, although I am unfamiliar with such extensive vistas. In fact, I feel almost a sense of vertigo. What is the source of the savage red glare?"

"That is the light of our ancient sun, now westering toward sunset."

"It does not appeal to me. Please be quick about your business; I have suddenly become most uneasy."

"I will make haste," said Cugel.

The sun, sinking low, sent a shaft of light through the portal, to play full upon the altar. Cugel, stepping behind the massive chair, twitched away the two shutters which guarded Phampoun's eyes, and the milky orbs glistened in the sunlight. For an instant Phampoun lay quiet. His muscles knotted, his legs jerked, his mouth gaped wide, and he emitted an explosion of sound: a grinding scream which propelled Pulsifer forth to vibrate like a flag in the wind. Phampoun lunged from the altar to fall sprawling and rolling across the floor of the temple, all the while maintaining his cataclysmic outcries. He pulled himself erect, and pounding the tiled floor with his great feet, he sprang here and there and at last burst through the stone walls as if they were paper, while the Kind Folk in the square stood petrified.

Cugel, taking the two sacks of gold, departed the temple by a side entrance. For a moment he watched Phampoun careering around the square, screaming and flailing at the sun. Pulsifer, desperately gripping a pair of tusks, attempted to steer the maddened demon, who, ignoring all restraint, plunged eastward through the city, trampling down trees, bursting through houses as if they failed to exist.

Cugel walked briskly down to the Isk and made his way out upon a dock. He selected a skiff of good proportions, equipped with mast, sail and oars, and prepared to clamber aboard. A punt approached the dock from upriver, poled vigorously by a large man in tattered garments. Cugel turned away, pretending no more than a casual interest in the view, until he might board the skiff without attracting attention.

The punt touched the dock; the boatman climbed up a ladder. Cugel continued to gaze across the water, affecting indifference to all except the river vistas.

The man, panting and grunting, came to a sudden halt. Cugel felt his intent inspection, and finally turning, looked into the congested face of Huruska, the Nolde of Gundar, though his face was barely recognizable for the bites Huruska had suffered from the insects of the Lallo Marsh.

Huruska stared long and hard at Cugel. "This is a most gratifying occasion!" he said huskily. "I feared that we would never meet again! The thought caused me more woe than I can explain. And what do you carry in those leather bags?" He wrested a bag from Cugel. "Gold from the weight. Your prophecy has been totally vindicated! First honors and a voyage by water, now wealth and revenge! Prepare to die!"

"One moment!" cried Cugel. "You have neglected properly to moor the punt! This is disorderly conduct!"

Huruska turned to look, and Cugel thrust him off the dock into the water.

Cursing and raving, Huruska struggled for the shore while Cugel fumbled with the knots in the mooring line of the skiff. The line at last came loose; Cugel pulled the skiff close as Huruska came charging down the dock like a bull. Cugel had no choice but to abandon his gold, jump into the skiff, push off and ply the oars while Huruska stood waving his arms in rage.

Cugel pensively hoisted the sail; the wind carried him down the river and around a bend. Cugel's last view of Lumarth, in the dying light of afternoon, included the low lustrous domes of the demon temples and the dark outline of Huruska standing on the dock. From afar the screams of Phampoun were still to be heard and occasionally the thud of toppling masonry.

Appendix:

THE YEAR'S BEST FANTASY BOOKS

I. ORIGINAL FICTION

1. *Watership Down,* by Richard Adams. Novel; 429 pp., $6.95; Macmillan. Would you believe a fantasy epic about rabbits on the top of *The New York Times* bestseller list? Well, this is it; and it's been compared to everything from *The Wind in the Willows* (because it anthropomorphizes its leporine characters, I suppose) to *The Lord of the Rings* (from its epic qualities).

2. *A Midsummer Tempest,* by Poul Anderson. Novel; 207 pp., $5.95; Doubleday. Charming Shakesperian fantasy set in a variant world in which Prospero and Oberon are real and all the characters (even the human ones) speak in blank verse. Anderson pulls it off rather nicely.

3. *Flashing Swords!* #2, edited by Lin Carter. Collection; 268 pp., 95¢, Dell. De Camp contributes a new Pusâdian tale, Moorcock a new Elric, Jakes a new Brak and Andre Norton a new Witch World novella, all four published here for the first time.

4. *The Warrior of World's End,* by Lin Carter. Novel; 160 pp., 95¢, map; DAW. First novel in a new

heroic fantasy series set on Earth hundreds of millions of years in the future, with magicians and gods and so on. A pinch of *The Dying Earth*, a spoonful of *Zothique*, and more than a dash of Oz.

5. *The Bull and the Spear*, by Michael Moorcock. Novel; 159 pp., 75¢; Berkley. First novel in a new series about Prince Corum; the sequels are *The Oak and the Ram, The Sword and the Stallion*. Rather grim and downbeat, but vivid and inventive.

6. *Merlin's Ring*, by H. Warner Munn. Novel; xi + 366 pp., maps, $1.95; Ballantine. Gigantic, panoramic Arthurian fantasy novel sprawling across centuries and continents. Robust and marvelous entertainment.

7. *The Jargoon Pard*, by Andre Norton. Novel; xii + 194 pp., $6.95; Atheneum. Ninth volume in this author's consistently entertaining Witch World series.

8. *A Quest for Simbilis*, by Michael Shea. Novel; 159 pp., 95¢; DAW. With permission, this new writer continues the adventures of Jack Vance's rogue, Cugel the Clever, on that author's Dying Earth. In the surprise of the year, he comes off a *very* close second to The Master himself. A stunning job, recommended without reservations.

9. *How are the Mighty Fallen*, by Thomas Burnett Swann. Novel; 160 pp., 95¢; DAW. Retelling of David and Goliath story which ties in with this author's favorite fantasy milieu, prehistoric Crete. Sensitively handled and oddly gripping, if a trifle slight.

10. *Prince of Annwn*, by Evangeline Walton. Novel; 179 pp., $1.50, Ballantine. With this novelized retelling of the First Branch of the mythological Welsh prose epic, one of the finest of living fantasy authors concludes her magnificent redaction of the mighty *Mabinogion*. Glorious!

II. IMPORTANT REPRINTS

11. *Over the Hills and Far Away*, by Lord Dunsany; edited, with introduction and notes, by Lin Carter. *xii* + 234 pp., $1.25, Ballantine. A third and final gleaning (under the Unicorn's Head colophon, anyway) from the tales, poems and plays of the greatest of all fantasy masters. Includes thirty-four stories rarely reprinted, plus a previously unknown and newly discovered tribute to Lord Dunsany by H. P. Lovecraft, which first appeared in my new fantasy magazine, *Kadath*.

12. *The People of the Black Circle*, by Robert E. Howard. 149 pp., numerous illu. in color and black-and-white by David Ireland, Donald M. Grant. Sumptuous deluxe hardcover edition of one of the major Conan stories: reportedly, the first of a new series of Conan yarns in collectors' editions. A beautiful job—tipped-in color plates, yet!

13. *The Lost Continent*, by C. J. Cutcliffe Hyne. *xiii* + 353 pp., $6.50, Oswald Train, PO Box 1891, Philadelphia, Pa. 19105. First hardcover printing of this classic in America since Harpers did it back in 1900. In case you didn't know, this is the best Atlantis novel of them all. With a new introduction by L. Sprague de Camp.

14. *The Metal Monster*, by A. Merritt. *xix* + 203 pp., $7.95, Hyperion. The first hardcover edition *ever* for this great fantasy masterpiece, although an incredibly sleazy job of printing and binding. New introduction by Sam Moskowitz.

15. *The Story of the Glittering Plain*, by William Morris. *xvi* + 174 pp., $1.95, Newcastle Publishing Co., 1521 North Vine, Hollywood, CA. 90028. Handsome, large-size paperback reprint of Morris' earliest (1890) fantastic romance, which Ballantine never got around to including in the Adult Fantasy Series. On a par with *The Sundering Flood*, which Ballantine did print.

16. *Grey Maiden,* by Arthur D. Howden Smith. 159 pp., $1.25, Centaur. History of a great sword down through the ages, and proof that the revival of classic fantasies will continue even though Ballantine has bowed out of the picture.

III. NOTEWORTHY NON-FICTION

17. *A Guide to Middle Earth,* by Robert Foster. *xiii* + 284 pp., $1.50, Ballantine. An absolutely incredible job of scholarship, this glossary-*cum*-concordance of every single proper noun in the entire Tolkien canon. I can't find an error or omission in it.

For better or for worse, these seventeen books seem to me the most important of all the fantasy novels or anthologies, books or brochures, from professional or fannish publishers, which came to my attention during 1974. You may disagree with my opinions, however, keep in mind that they are only *my* opinions.

To make certain that *your* book or books are seen and considered for this honor roll in next year's *Year's Best Fantasy,* send your publications to me, care of DAW Books, Inc.

Everything forwarded to me for my consideration will be read and adjudged. More than that I cannot promise.

Happy Magic for 1975!

LIN CARTER